Ordinary Murder

Ordinary Murder

Don Flynn

Walker and Company
New York

First published in the United States of America
in 1987 by the Walker Publishing Company, Inc.

Published simultaneously in Canada by Thomas Allen & Son
Canada, Limited, Markham, Ontario.

Library of Congress Cataloging-in-Publication Data

Flynn, Don.
    Ordinary murder.

    I. Title.
PS3556.L8407   1987   813'.54   87-18896
ISBN 0-8027-5687-5

Printed in the United States of America

10 9 8 7 6 5 4 3 2 1

For JOHN PASCAL

New York newspaperman.

Ordinary Murder

1

"A MAN MUST stand erect, not be held erect by others," advises the wise ancient Roman emperor Marcus Aurelius. It was a maxim James Kelly never understood and that his father, Timmy, never had to be taught. James's lack of understanding left him shot to death one morning in his Upper East Side co-op in Manhattan, and caused me more grief than I care to remember. Because Timmy was my friend.

Actually I didn't know James very well at the time he was killed. Sometimes you only get to know a person after he's dead. You have to find out about him from other people, of course, and it's all frozen in the past. And sometimes, you learn things you might just as soon not have known.

I knew his father Timmy from Kelly's, a bar he runs on Third Avenue down the street from the *Daily Press* on Forty-second Street. When you're a newspaper reporter in New York City, you seem to wind up in bars once in a while. When somebody wants to give you the greatest story in the world, which is often, they take you to Costello's or P.J. Clarke's or Sardi's. And even when there were no devious press agents or politicians to drag me into a place, I sometimes found such places on my own. And when I did, it was usually Timmy's. Officially, it was the New Dublin Inne, but it was Kelly's to us.

I don't want you to think a newspaperman spends all his time in bars. It's just that people invite you in, or maybe even coerce you. I can remember times when four NFL linemen dragged me into low saloons and forced grog down my gullet until I believed myself to be *Scipio africanus*. I could never find or identify those thoughtless bullies the next morning when I stood before Ironhead Matthews, my city editor, trying waveringly to explain my piteous condition.

Anyway, that's why I knew Timmy. Kelly's is an authentic old New York bar, like the traditional Dublin or London pub, with aged wood and photographs of Jack Dempsey and Jimmy Walker on the walls, and a pleasantly gloomy atmosphere of camaraderie. It's the kind of place where a temporarily tapped-out reporter could sign a tab, or give Timmy Kelly a check, and ask him to hold it until Monday. And if it bounced, Timmy would only bellow that I was a "durty Irish deadbeat," and send it through again. I don't want to hear a lot of snide remarks about it, because none of my checks ever bounced more than once as far as I can remember.

I was at my desk in the city room of the *Daily Press* that morning, waiting for Ironhead to give me an assignment, when the call came in.

"Fitz," said a voice full of anxiety.

"Yeah."

"Timmy Kelly." He paused a second, and I could sense the trouble in him.

"What's the matter, Timmy?"

Still he waited. Then, "You know anybody at the Nineteenth Precinct?"

"I don't know, off hand, Timmy. Why?"

"It's James . . ."

"What happened?"

I was beginning to think Timmy wasn't on the line any longer. But at last he spoke again, a barely audible whisper. "Fitz . . . Jesus . . . Fitz, my boy's dead."

I sank onto the chair at my desk, and an elevator

2

plummeted downward inside me. Now I was the one who couldn't speak.

"Christ, Timmy," I finally managed. "I'm sorry."

"Sure, I know you are, Fitz," he said then, his voice a little steadier. The worst words were out of him, but there were more to come, still not easy to say. "I had to go identify my boy, Fitz . . . they shot him."

A long breath came out of me. "They? What's it about, Timmy, do you know?"

"No, Fitz. That's why I called you. Find out for me, will you? I'm half crazy, and . . . how am I gonna tell Edna?"

I didn't envy him that frightful duty. "I'll see what I can do," I said. "Where are you?"

"Home. I just got back. I was up there making the identification."

"What's your number there? I'll call you."

"No, Fitz, don't call. Edna might answer. I'll call you back later . . . unless you could stop by here." He gave me his address out in Bay Ridge in Brooklyn.

"I'll get back to you," I told him.

I hung up the phone and stared into nothingness. Sometimes it's a problem being a reporter. People think of you as an insider who knows everybody and how to find out things they can't. Well, you are an insider to some degree, it's true, but it's mostly bluff because you have no gun or police shield or legal leverage. You have to pursue a nosey stubborness against a vague, indifferent criminal justice system that responds only when constantly poked.

I realized, of course, that the routine thing was to call Dubbs Brewer at the *Daily Press* police bureau downtown and ask him to check it out for me. It wasn't the kind of story that Ironhead would send anyone out to cover. Getting killed isn't a big story in New York City any more. Not when there are more than 1,600 murders

3

a year—or about 4.5 per day. So unless the victim is a state senator keeping a go-go dancer on the side, or one of these androgynous rock stars that the kids had elevated to celebrity freaks, another murder draws little attention.

I walked over to the city desk, where Ironhead was beslobbering his greasy cigar and glowering at the morning's stack of press releases, handouts, tips, memos, and the city side news schedule of murders, robberies, subway muggings and political press conferences, the usual gory detritus of the Big Apple.

"Ironhead," I started.

He gave me a swift, frowning glance, and went back to his stack of what he always called "the morning garbage."

"Yeah?" he snapped, still riffling papers.

"You know Timmy who runs Kelly's bar down the street?"

"What?" He didn't look up.

"Listen, his son's been murdered, and I wonder if I could go have a look."

"Goddam garbage," he muttered irritably. Ironhead was once slugged by a nightstick while covering a riot as a young reporter, and I believe it affected his already lopsided personality and turned him into an ascerbic troglodyte, which resulted inevitably in his becoming city editor.

Anyway, he suddenly looked up at me again, as though noticing me for the first time, and said, "What are you working on, Fitz?"

"I just got a call from Timmy, who runs Kelly's bar down on Third Avenue. His son's been murdered, and I was going to go have a look."

"Timmy Kelly?" he asked, and gave a little tisk, tisk city editor shake of his head. "Too bad. Anything unusual about it?"

"I don't know yet."

"Well, let Dubbs check that out." He picked up a sheet of paper on which he had scribbled some indecipherable notes. "Houseman's got an idea for a series here, and I've got nobody else free to handle it."

I'm afraid I swayed back and frowned. It's always a blunder to walk into the city editor's field of vision just after he's been given a wonderful new series idea by the managing editor.

"It's up at the Nineteenth," I tried.

"What is?"

"James Kelly's murder."

Ironhead turned around to look at the hieroglyphics on his sheet of paper. "Now, Fitz, Houseman wants a series about Manhattan's buildings."

"Buildings . . . ?"

Yes, it seemed that Bill Houseman had been driving to Manhattan from his home in Westchester County and had been smitten with a fresh discovery. The Manhattan skyline! It was glorious, he realized, it was the signature of the Big Apple, it was . . . *romantic!* . . . and it was being ignored.

It turned out that the evening before his vision Houseman had had dinner at the Union League Club with our publisher, Mr. McFadden, and Mr. McFadden had mused plaintively over his Pouilly Fuissé and lobster thermidor about the scandalous lack of coverage of our man-made Ninth Wonders of the World. To wit: our skyscrapers. Not surprisingly, Houseman had been promptly smitten with his idea, which was to publish a rhapsodic paean to the Manhattan skyline.

Houseman had even given Ironhead the title for the series.

"What we want is a goddam series called The Romance of Buildings," Ironhead informed me, his mouth sort of going down at the corners as he got it out.

I sank into a chair across from him at the city desk and lighted a Tiparillo, trying frantically to think of a way out.

"What about Timmy Kelly's son?" I said hopefully.

The irascible city editor lowered his sheet of doodles and turned a perplexed face on me. "Haven't you heard a word I've said here?"

"Well, sure, but I'm working on a murder."

"You're working on what I say you're working on!"

Oh.

"It sounds like an ordinary murder, anyway."

"A series about *buildings*?" I muttered with less enthusiasm than was wise.

"Yes, goddamit!" Ironhead's antennae were always tuned to unfortunate shows of lack of spirit. "Buildings! The city's full of them, if you haven't noticed, and nobody knows they're there."

"But you can *see* them."

Never mind that, Ironhead leaped onward. It was time the buildings of Manhattan were brought to the attention of our readers.

"Which ones?" I asked rather limply in a foot-dragging manner.

"Goddamit, look out the window," he said. The truth was, of course, that Ironhead knew it was a crackbrained idea, but he had no choice but to be enthusiastic and defend it.

"You mean just any building?"

I had made a blunder. I had dawdled too long asking embarrassing questions, and what I got for it was Old Faithful erupting.

Any dim-witted ninnyhammer of a cub reporter from the goddam *Bronx Home News* could find buildings in Manhattan! There was Rockefeller Center, the Empire State Building, red and gold pagodas in Chinatown decorated with dragons, the World Trade Center, the goddam Chrysler Building! Was I blind? Could I find my way to Times Square?

"I realize that, back in St. Louis or East Outhouse, Iowa, or wherever the hell you come from, they have nothing but pig pens and roadside potato stands! But this is New York! Go out and find a goddam building!"

I slunk away. It was a mistake to goad Ironhead on a subject that made him see red.

When I got back to my desk, Bike O'Malley was beaming. He had heard it all.

"Fitz, it's the chance of a lifetime."

"Up yours."

"I understand there's a building on Seventh Avenue."

Well, that's when I got my bright idea. It suddenly occurred to me in a blinding flash that police stations were buildings, too. Everybody had heard about Rockefeller Center, but how about a paean of praise to the Nineteenth Precinct? I wish I could tell you that I realized at the time that this would cause ambivalent sensations in Ironhead's inflamed skull.

2

I LEFT THE city room and walked to my dusty, maroon 1978 Mustang in the NYP parking zone behind the *Daily Press*. I had picked it up recently from Nick Fiske, a rewrite man, after my 1969 Ford Falcon had been totaled in front of the Tenth Precinct. Don't even ask about that, because it's too painful to go into. I was being chased by a Neanderthal thug killer, and had to stop and back into him to get away. Ironhead could never discuss that incident rationally, because he always ended up shrieking that you don't get away from somebody by backing into a Lincoln and crashing into a lot of police cars. But I'm not going to go into it.

The Mustang was quite spiffy, if you were Fiske's teenage son. It had these hubcaps that looked like plates upon which Augustus Caesar would serve banquets. And the rear end was humped upward on special springs, so I always felt I was going downhill. There were also a lot of gleaming tubes under the back end that gave off a thunderous vrooming. I was going to get it remodeled into an ordinary car as soon as I could stop by John the Chevron man's place on Second Avenue. I had already removed the two oversized dice that had hung from the rearview mirror in front of my eyes.

I admit I sometimes have trouble with cars, but at the moment the Mustang was humming like a finely tuned jet engine. Except that it sometimes sounded as though it were taking off from Kennedy airport.

I drove uptown to the Nineteenth Precinct, which is on the Upper East Side of Manhattan, a neighborhood known as the Silk Stocking District because it includes some first-class real estate and a lot of wealthy people. Sutton Place is in the Nineteenth, for instance. It runs from Fifth Avenue to the East River between Fifty-ninth and Eighty-sixth Streets. Actually, my apartment on East Eighty-second Street is in the Nineteenth, but that only shows there are also some wrinkled socks in the Silk Stocking District. If I hadn't moved into my joint a few years ago when rents were lower, I probably couldn't get in now.

Anyway, the Nineteenth Precinct station house is on East Sixty-seventh Street across from the Soviet Union United Nations Mission, and that's where I headed that morning after Timmy called me with a voice full of misery, and I had rationalized myself into the idea of the romance of police stations.

You can't tell the inside of a police station by the district it's in, for all that. They all look the same, whether it's the Silk Stocking District or Ralph Avenue in Brooklyn. There isn't a lot of romance about them, to tell the truth. You walk in and find a rather nondescript big room with an upraised desk and a scowling sergeant behind it.

"Morning, Sarge," I offered. "Fitzgerald, *Daily Press.*"

The sergeant's face twitched a lttle at that. When reporters walk in, they all react that way. "Now what?" is the message you get.

"Yeah?" he said, putting up a wall.

"Sarge, you got anything on somebody named James Kelly?"

"What about him?"

"Murder victim."

The sarge frowned and narrowed his eyes. Then he made a face and glanced at a cop sitting at another desk. "Got anything on a Kelly?" the sarge asked him. "See if there's an unusual." Then, to me, "When did it happen?"

"Last night or early this morning, I think."

The desk cop got up and came closer to the sergeant and spoke softly to him, handing him a slip of paper. The sergeant read it over, glancing at me over the top.

"Yeah," he said. "Okay. The squad's got it. Messina's still at the scene."

"Where's the scene?"

The sergeant glanced at the paper again. "Let's see . . ." He gave me a number on East Sixty-sixth.

"Thanks," I said, and walked back outside and down a block to Sixty-sixth Street.

The apartment building, just off Lexington Avenue, had a stylish, green scalloped canopy out over the sidewalk, and a big curved lobby with some kind of orange and blue modernistic artwork on the walls. I checked the listings and saw a J. Kelly on the third floor. The uniformed doorman looked at my press card and pushed a button that let sliding glass doors open before me. The building was one of those places that had gone co-op a few years earlier when real estate dealers figured out this wonderful way to force tenants to buy already overpriced apartments at inflated rates.

I rode up in the elevator to three, and when I stepped out there were cops in the corridor. I walked over.

"Fitzgerald, *Daily Press*."

The uniformed cop looked at me, and then called into the apartment. "Hey, Messina. The press."

I walked in past the cop, who didn't try to stop me. Detective Messina was coming toward me. A dark-faced, slightly beefy guy with a bent nose, suspicious brown

10

eyes and a wide tie with red and black crisscrossed lines on it.

"Detective Messina," he said noncommittally.

"Hi. Fitzgerald, *Daily Press*." We looked at each other. "Can you tell me anything?" I ventured.

Messina took out a little notebook, opened it, and let me have it. "Male, white, twenty-seven. Tentative ID James Kelly."

I glanced past him and saw a chalk silhouette drawn on the rug near a desk. The outline resembled a person drawn up in a fetal position, as though he were clutching his middle.

"That's where he got it?" I asked.

Messina took out a large cigar and lighted it, studying me. "The ME removed the body about an hour ago," he said.

I walked over a little closer to the desk and stood with my hands behind me.

"Doesn't look like much for you guys," Messina went on.

"No. I knew him."

"Oh. Well, then, maybe you can help me," said Messina, sinking into a chair beside a marble coffee table. "What do you know about him?"

It was a good question. That's when I first realized how little I really knew about James.

"His father runs a bar on Third Avenue," I started. "Kelly's. Actually, it's the New Dublin Inne."

Messina was making notes in his little log book.

"I think he was in real estate," I went on, culling my memory for bits that Timmy had dropped when I wasn't really paying much attention.

"Yeah," said Messina. "That's what I understood. You know who he worked for?"

"Uh . . . no."

"What else?" he asked me, his pen poised over his pad.

My well was pretty dry. "He went to Amherst," I offered.

"What?" Messina didn't bother to write that down.

"Yeah. Played tennis."

"Tennis?"

"His father lives out in Bay Ridge."

At least he took that down. Then he turned his bent nose on me and waited for more. But I had run out my skimpy string.

"Can you tell me anything about how it happened?" I asked instead.

"All I know right now is that somebody shot him."

"When?"

"Don't know exactly. Early this morning sometime."

"Got any ideas?"

Messina obviously wasn't going to give away the moon. "We've got some leads," he said laconically.

"Such as?"

"They're under investigation."

"Any motive?"

"Not really."

I felt frustrated. Detective Messina either didn't like reporters or was cautious to the point of silence. "Can't you fill me in a little?" I tried again. "I told you all I knew."

His eyebrows went up. "*You* told me? You don't seem to know this guy from Adam."

"Well, for chrissake, can't you give me some details? Where was he hit? How many times? Any suspects? I have to talk to his father."

That seemed to soften bent-nose Messina a bit. He scowled defiantly, but took out his little notebook again. "You guys are supposed to go through public information downtown," he grumbled. Which is true, in the new

Police Department. But guys like me, who've been around awhile, usually go to the source if we can.

"Come on, Messina," I nudged, "give a little, will ya?"

Well, Messina finally dropped a few tidbits. James had been hit three times in the body from very close with a high-powered handgun.

"Probably a nine millimeter," he said.

"Anybody hear the shots? Who found him?"

"We got a tip to check this apartment," he said rather grudgingly.

"Who tipped you?"

Messina folded his notebook and put it back into his jacket pocket. That was all I was going to get at the moment.

It told me something, though. A nine millimeter automatic will put a slug through a concrete block, and at close range is a devastating weapon.

Whoever got James wasn't fooling around.

3

I WALKED OUT of the apartment building and back up to the Nineteenth, where my Mustang was parked. Heading down Lexington Avenue to go out to Brooklyn, I was wondering what I could say to Timmy.

The way it is in New York with reporters and bar owners is that you show affection by breaking each other's shoes. Timmy always ragged me about being broke, which is the normal condition of the ink-stained wretches of the Fourth Estate.

"Fitz," Timmy used to ask me with an elaborate, florid-faced sigh, "what do you do with all your *munney?*"

"Timmy," I would say, "it's a mystery, but a reporter doesn't have 'all your money' in the first place."

"Humph," Kelly would snort contemptuously, "my father saved enough working as a hod carrier to open this bar, and he was no overpaid, hotshot *noospaper* reporter."

"Yes, Timmy, your father was a paragon of thrift and virtue. So how did his son turn out to be a pain in the grumper?"

"Fitzgerald, you're full of canal water."

"More beer and less stale drivel."

Tim would stomp down the bar grumbling and draw me a mug of draft Harp beer. If he broke my shoes too much, I would ask about what he had running at Aqueduct, and that would get him going on his horse bets. So much for all that thrift, by the way.

Timmy's father, Liam, had started Kelly's a few years after he had come over from Dublin, and it had been a fixture for, I don't know, fifty years or something. By now the old block had begun to deteriorate. Some of the old brick buildings were being torn down and others were boarded up, awaiting the wrecker's ball. A few crumbling tenements still stood on the block, inhabited by welfare people and street characters, some of whom frequented the bar, to Timmy's grumbling disapproval.

Along with the deterioration of the block and the arrival of the scruffy street element came other troubles as well.

I remember Timmy glancing past me and frowning in annoyance. "Ah, me, they're back again," he mumbled. I looked around and two men in cheap suits were coming in. "Now what do they want?" he asked no one in particular.

"What's the matter?"

"Ah, the devil," said Timmy. "Inspectors again! A regular plague of them lately. Imagine, they want bannisters on the cellar stairs! As if any customers go down there." He walked off down the bar to do battle with the inspectors.

He had gotten a new landlord, too, and had been pressured for a while to give up his lease. But he had held on, convinced the new landlord that nothing would get him out, and the new property owners had eventually stopped bothering him.

He wouldn't give up the family business because he felt the neighborhood would come back, as they always do eventually in Manhattan. And he had someone to pass the place on to.

Bay Ridge is out in Brooklyn, down by the Narrows. You go over the Brooklyn Bridge and then south down the Brooklyn-Queens Expressway and along the elevated Gowanus Expressway past the old piers of Bush Terminal and then down into Bay Ridge along Fourth Avenue. Bay Ridge is an Irish neighborhood that has held up over the years, maintaining its middle-class residential character pretty well, unlike Fort Hamilton on the north and Coney Island further out. I found Timmy's house on Seventy-third Street off Fourth Avenue, a tan limestone attached place with a little, well-kept lawn in front.

I sat in the Mustang and smoked a Tiparillo, trying to work up the courage to go in. It was curious to feel the neighborhood around me where James had grown up. I kept wondering how James's path after Bay Ridge and Amherst had led to what Timmy always called admiringly "the uptown people" and finally to that chalked silhouette on the rug.

I got out of the car and walked to Tim Kelly's sand-colored limestone house. Iron railings on the small concrete porch. I didn't even have to touch the lighted doorbell panel beside the front door. Timmy opened the door and looked at me, his face a mask of unspoken fear and resignation. I walked in.

Inside, the house was what my grandmother used to call "close." It was half-darkened, for one thing, and crammed with furniture so that you could hardly walk. Carpeting muffled your footsteps, and there was an oppressive stale-air atmosphere. There were photographs and little statues and knickknacks everywhere. It suggested the house of an invalid.

"Come in, come in," Timmy said with a nervous show of welcome. "Sit down. What can I get you?"

I walked into the cluttered living room and sank into a large green couch. Timmy stood across from me behind a coffee table on which there were plants growing out of a swan ornament and a rectangular bronze planter. He wasn't able to look at me.

16

"A drink?" he asked, going through the ritual of welcome that held off whatever bad news I had brought for a few moments longer.

"No, thanks."

Then Timmy stepped backward and sat in a chair. He looked at me straight, his eyes unblinking but nervous.

"What can you tell me?" he asked softly.

I told him the few facts I had gotten from bent-nose Messina.

Timmy shook his head. "Three times," he said flatly. "It must have been quick, then."

I nodded. "Yeah."

"The bastards!"

"I'm sorry," I finally muttered.

"Ah, Jesus," he said then. "How will I ever tell Edna?" How indeed? He rose suddenly and walked out of the room. I sat there like a rock, unable to move or react. In a moment he was back with a bottle of Irish whiskey and two glasses. He poured drinks into both of them, and took one himself.

Timmy took a strong gulp and leaned forward, staring at what I don't know—probably the past and a boy coming home from school. Looking into those far-away eyes, I saw no wise-cracking Manhattan bar owner but an ordinary, aging man who accepted what he had to but did not always pretend to understand.

"Have ya got one of those weeds?" he asked. I gave him a slim Tiparillo cigar, which he unwrapped slowly and lit. "Where is he?"

I gave him the number of the Medical Examiner's office so he could make arrangements to claim the body. When he asked if they knew who had done it, I had to shake my head "no."

"You got any ideas?" I asked Timmy. "What was he doing?"

Timmy puffed on the Tiparillo and wagged his head

back and forth slowly, trying to assimilate the enormity of it all.

"You got any ideas of what could have happened?" I repeated tentatively.

Timmy sat there like a stone, and his eyes were red and watery. "Ah, God," he muttered once. Then he turned around, took out a handkerchief, and blew his nose.

"Sorry, Fitz," he murmured, and my heart went out to him.

After that, Timmy tried to think. "He was working in real estate up there on Sixth Avenue," he told me. "Had a big job, you know."

I sipped the Irish whiskey Timmy had given me and tried not to react. You know how it is when a close friend brags lovingly about his son or daughter and you don't share the feeling? Timmy naturally doted on James and could see no flaws in him. But I could not imagine James having a big job—in real estate or anyplace else.

"Real estate?" I finally asked, keeping my thoughts to myself. What else could I do?

"Yep." Timmy was taking comfort from his words. "He was doing fine. He just bought a co-op apartment, and you know they don't come cheap."

"Yeah," I said, and remembered the place I had been in, with the marble coffee table and the bar and the giant TV screen.

"Do you know what he paid for it?" I asked.

"He told me about a hundred grand," said Timmy without showing much surprise. A lot of pride, yes, but not much surprise. But it bowled me over.

"That much?" I asked.

"Sure," said Timmy. "And he had a new car, too. I think I've got one of his cards here someplace."

Timmy went to an old rolltop desk in the corner and

dug through pigeonholes and little drawers, looking for the card. I was in a brown study, trying to make sense of what he had told me.

James Kelly buying a $100,000 co-op and a new car? I couldn't imagine it.

Then Timmy was back with the business card, a tastefully printed oblong with embossed letters: "Magen & Burke, Real Estate Brokers & Managers, 1274 Sixth Avenue."

I looked at the card. "You think James made the money at this place?"

"Why sure," said Timmy. "The boy always did have the gift of gab, you know that."

Yes, I knew that. But James's gab was usually unconnected with anything substantial.

"Was he in any kind of trouble?" I asked.

"Not that I knew about," he said sadly, stepping gingerly around a painful subject. "I hadn't seen him much after he left the store."

I had almost forgotten about that. Timmy was talking about the time last summer when James briefly took over Kelly's.

"What did he do after that?" I asked.

"I guess he went back to real estate," he said.

A faint, quavering call. "Timothy."

Timmy stiffened and stood up immediately. He looked toward the back of the house. "Yes, Edna!"

"Is somebody there?"

"It's all right." He wagged his great, florid head slowly, his face a seamed picture of despair. "I'll never be able to tell her."

"Anything I can do, Tim?"

Timmy Kelly shot a glance at me then, filled with rage and frustration. "Yes, Fitz! Find out what happened!

Ride the cops till they get them! Don't let me down, Edward.''

I think it was the only time in his life he ever called me that.

4

"A MAN IS worth just as much as the things about which he busies himself," says Marcus Aurelius. "When you are offended with any man's shameless conduct, immediately ask youself, 'Is it possible that there should be no shameless men in the world?' It is not possible. Do not, therefore, require what is impossible."

Marcus's words were running through my head as I drove back to Manhattan thinking about James. I was, like Don Quixote de la Mancha, embarked upon an impossible quest, I thought wistfully. Because I was afraid that in trying to bring Timmy some peace by finding out what happened to James, I might find out things that might hurt him more than his son's death.

I think the reason I didn't know James very well was because I had blocked him out of my consciousness. He used to pop into Kelly's once in a while, carrying a tennis racket and giving the impression that he was just down from the New York Athletic Club—or maybe had just flown in on the Concorde. He would touch Timmy for cash, and then be off on his rounds. I always had the feeling he would quip, "Tennis, anyone?" on the way out.

The thing is, I felt that James never respected his father, and only spoke civilly to him when he wanted money. "Nothing is more disgraceful than a wolfish friendship," said Marcus.

I know it was unfair of me to think these things about

James before I knew anything very much about him. But I believe in instinct, and I had a feeling about James I couldn't shake.

You know how it is when you meet a guy from Brooklyn who wants to forget where he came from? That's the way James had always struck me. He went to Amherst College and met a lot of Waspy kids, and when he came back to New York he didn't want to remember that his father and his father before him had been saloon keepers.

Timmy used to tell me he was holding Kelly's for James, and that as soon as James finished college he would start learning the business. When Timmy talked about it, he would go into his routine about retiring to Florida.

"Edna wants to feed the pelicans," he had told me, looking rather baffled.

"Pelicans?"

"That's exactly what I asked her," Timmy had said. Why pelicans? Well, it seems when Edna visited her cousin Mai down there on the Keys, there were all these daffy pelicans flopping around. Cousin Mai had even given the brazen things names! He had stared out toward Third Avenue. "Never been out on the Keys myself."

"I thought you and Edna went down all the time."

Timmy's face had gotten red and he had made a face. "Well, now, Fitz, we have. But I seem to stop off at Hialeah for a day or so to visit my brother while Edna goes down to the pelicans, and by the time I'm ready to join her it's time to come back."

"Hialeah, huh?"

"No lectures, you deadbeat. Have a beer." He slid a mug of Harp over the bar. "Can you picture it? Pelicans eating out of Edna's hand? Why, they have great whooping jaws like a hippopotamus."

Well, when James got out of college and came back to New York, he didn't want anything to do with the bar.

There Timmy had been holding the place for James, turning down offers to sell out, and James wasn't interested.

Of course, James wasn't the first son who ever showed no interest in something his father had spent a lifetime building. But it hurt Timmy.

"Why don't you sell the joint?" James would say, lounging in a back booth in his Irish handsomeness and unthinking, sophomoric cruelty. "I'm not working here six days a week, twelve hours a day."

"This place made a living for my father, and for me and Edna, and you, too," Timmy would splutter. "It'll be yours one day. I've been holding it for you."

"Don't hold your breath, Pop."

But James had a change of heart eventually, and he did finally take over Kelly's for a while.

Let me tell you, he was no Timmy. Timmy walked around in shirtsleeves, wearing a plain tie with a Holy Name Society tie-clasp, and everybody thought of him as the bartender. Not James.

James Kelly, bless the saints, wore blue banker's pinstriped suits and seventy-dollar Sulka ties, and he fit into Kelly's like a preacher in a massage parlor. And, equally predictable, the irreverent types who hang out there called him everything except James. "Squirt" and "Big Shot" were among the mildest terms. And Bike O'Malley called him "Cobby."

Once, James pulled me aside and asked bewilderedly what "Cobby" could possibly mean. I explained that certain ill-mannered reporters called people "Cobby" to suggest that the person in question walked as though he had a corn cob stuffed up his grumper.

James's rather impassive, aristocratic Ivy League face went red and he glared at me as though *I* were one of those ill-mannered wretches.

Well, some of the reporters simply drifted away, back

up to Costello's or Ryan-McFadden's or Louie's East behind the *Daily Press* building. But some of us stayed on, out of loyalty to Timmy and because we were too lazy to worry about it.

James strutted around in his corn-cob stiff walk and styled red hair and tried to put the best face on it he could. His every movement, word, and expression made it clear that he was suffering through a distressing purgatory, as though he were a Rockefeller drafted into the army as a private, or a first-class passenger who had somehow unaccountably been put in economy.

Sometimes, some of James's Sulka tie friends would come in and sit with him in the back booth, where they would watch us all, as though they were slumming at P.T. Barnum's Museum. I particularly remember a glorious woman who came in a few times and sat at the back table, her legs agonizingly visible under the table. Sculptured black hair and a creamy Celtic face. Lace-curtain Irish all the way.

Anyway, the whole thing was a disaster. It just didn't work out. Timmy bent my ear plenty at the time, telling me James would drive the store out of business in six months. So he decided to keep the place and said he'd offer it to James again in a few years, after he'd "grown up a little." And in any event, James would get it after he was gone.

Oddly enough, James had been really put out about it. I had thought he didn't really want the bar, but apparently he did. He and Timmy had words about it.

"Dad, you don't under*stand*," James had ranted. "I've already made plans."

"That's good," Timmy had said calmly. "Plans are important. Your plans will still be good later on after you've learned more about the saloon business."

"But it's too late," James had pleaded. "And I don't give a damn about the saloon business."

24

"I know. That's why I'm keeping the place, for now."

James had finally given up and had drifted back uptown, apparently back into what Timmy always called proudly "the real estate game."

"He wasn't right for the store," Timmy told me with a sigh, and who could quarrel with that?

After that, I hadn't seen or heard any more about James until Timmy had called me.

5

I WISH I COULD tell you I had the slightest idea of how to pursue James Kelly's murder. What I hoped was that Detective Messina would solve the damn thing and get it off my back.

I drifted back to the *Daily Press* and was sitting at my desk in the city room, puffing on a Tiparillo and looking for an idea. I was searching for something that didn't add up, and what I came up with was that it didn't make sense for James to quit a big job in real estate to take over his father's bar. Of course, it didn't make sense that James had a big job—in real estate or anything else—to begin with. That is, it didn't make sense to me. It made sense to Timmy.

"I don't give a damn about the saloon business," James had said. But he had taken over Kelly's. Why?

A dark shape materialized beside me as I pondered, and gradually faded into my consciousness.

"Got any kind of handle on it yet?" the dark shape asked me. Ironhead stood there chewing on his slimy cigar.

"Not really," I confessed.

"What have you considered so far?"

"Why he left Magen & Burke, mostly."

"What?"

"He doesn't care about Kelly's, so why did he take it over?"

Ironhead shuffled his feet and frowned. "Why did *who* take over what?"

"I guess the lead will have to be that he was shot in his fancy apartment and there's no apparent motive."

"No *motive?*"

"Not that I can figure out. Messina's working on some leads, but there are no suspects yet."

"What the hell are you talking about?"

"James Kelly's murder."

Ironhead's head jerked back as though he had been splashed by a passing car. Then it came forward again. He shook his head like a dog coming out of a pond. "What about the buildings?"

Oh, that.

"Well, I've been looking some over," I said, trying to switch gears.

"You have, huh?" Ironhead seemed doubtful. "Which ones?"

"See, I thought it would be a different kind of angle if I included some unusual buildings. I went and had a look at the Nineteenth Precinct station house, and—"

"A *police station* building?" Ironhead's face went into a pained sort of grimace. "You consider a police station part of the Manhattan skyline?"

"Well . . ."

"You think Mr. McFadden wants a series about the romance of police stations!" His annoyance slid over into angry red splotches and a throbbing vein in his forehead.

"You probably never noticed that the lights in front of a precinct house are purple."

". . . *purple?* . . ."

"Maybe I can leave the precincts out. But as long as I was there, can you use a fat box about James Kelly's murder?"

Ironhead's mouth came open and sort of froze. His jaw worked and his eyes narrowed. "Goddamit!"

"I'll keep it tight," I said hurriedly. "And then I'll get right on the building series."

"See that you do," Ironhead muttered, and stalked back to the city desk.

I wrote what we call a fat box—three paragraphs—which was about all I could hope to get in about what Ironhead had rightly called an ordinary murder.

There really wasn't much more I could do after that, except wait to see what Detective Messina came up with.

Most murders are solved right away or not at all. You have the maddened husband who stalks into the estranged wife's office and shoots her in front of a dozen screaming office workers, or the crazed kid who wipes out his family with a shotgun. But a body found in an apartment with few clues and no suspects very often goes unsolved unless the killer turns himself in, or unless somebody drops a dime on the guy. That's what the cops call it when somebody drops a coin into a pay phone and calls the police to turn somebody in. Of course, with the new pay phones in Manhattan, it costs a quarter to drop a dime on somebody now. Anyway, detectives in a case like James Kelly's murder will probably solve it within forty-eight hours if they're going to solve it at all.

When I had finished the fat box, Ironhead waved me back over to the city desk, apparently having decided that I needed a little guidance.

"Look," he hissed softly, "Houseman was over here this morning and asked if we're going to include the Chamber of Commerce in the series."

"The Chamber of Commerce?"

"They've got a building downtown some place," Ironhead explained.

"Oh, yeah. Where is it?"

"How the hell do *I* know! Find it."

The next morning I awoke filled with sincere plans to go downtown and find the Chamber of Commerce Building, but as I was putting my press card into my jacket, I came across that business card Timmy had given me.

I could drive across town and check out the real estate firm on the way, I decided, which seemed a harmless enough idea at the time.

The address for Magen & Burke was an immense, glass box of a building on Sixth Avenue, a little north of Radio City Music Hall. I parked in an NYP zone and walked up Sixth, noticing the great canyon of buildings stretching away northward to Central Park. Manhattan certainly is a wonder. Houseman was right about that, and it was kind of true that you hardly even notice it most of the time. Great monoliths, with shelves of glass, and sunlight playing on the different levels, march north and south, east and west.

When you live and work in Manhattan, you experience the bizarre sensation of walking around a corner and suddenly seeing a sixty-story building you've never noticed before. They're always tearing things down and putting things up. Somebody once remarked that "New York will be a great city, if they ever finish it." Of course, they never will.

The emperor Augustus once said about ancient Rome, "I found Rome built of bricks, and I leave her clothed in marble." Somebody will say one day that the builders found New York built of bricks but left it clothed in glass.

The lobby of Magen & Burke's building was an immense Kublai Kahn showplace with a fountain and a carved marble bust of somebody on a pillar. I rode up in the elevator inside the great monolith to the thirty-second-floor offices of the real estate firm and came to swinging glass double doors with the name on the front in gold Bodoni Bold. Through the doors into the real estate office, and into a flossy, carpeted suite with chrome furniture, a blonde, vinyl-covered receptionist, and two huge potted plants.

I checked the business card, and the president was listed as Konrad Magen. There was no Burke on the card, and I wondered what had happened to him—or her. I asked to see Konrad Magen.

"Who shall I say is here?" she wanted to know.

"Ed Fitzgerald, *Daily Press*."

The blonde punched the phone buttons with lacquered nails, and spoke to somebody. Then she smiled up at me and said in her vinyl-covered voice, "Won't you please have a seat?"

I sat in a sprawling, curved sofa by the plate-glass windows looking out over Sixth Avenue, and thumbed a copy of *Fortune,* something I seldom have occasion to look into.

After a while, the lacquered blonde waved me over to her desk and said she would show me in now. We walked in through two glass doors that slid open before us, and I followed her along a white-walled corridor to the large, sunny corner office of Konrad Magen.

"Mr. Fitzgerald," Magen said, standing to shake hands across the corner of his desk. He was a smooth-looking executive with a powerful chest and determined eyes. He looked as though he could have been an NFL cornerback a few years ago.

He waved me to a large, executive gray sofa and then went back behind his great expanse of desk to sit watching me expectantly.

In front of me was a glistening scale model of a building about four feet high that Magen & Burke apparently had in their crystal ball. All glass and chrome, like so many other new buildings going up in Manhattan. I remember I had wondered aloud once why they don't build of brick or stone anymore, and Timmy Kelly—whose father had been a hod carrier—set me straight:

"They won't pay for bricklayers anymore, so they use glass."

Across the bottom of the model were the proud words The Magen Building.

I gestured toward the Magen Building model and said, "Something you're putting up?" hoping to break the ice a little.

Konrad Magen's determined eyes softened, and he smiled, standing up behind his desk and coming around to pause reverently before the glass model.

"Yes . . . the Magen Building," he said proudly. "It's been a dream of mine ever since I came to New York from Paterson as a kid."

"Impressive," I said, but he hardly heard me.

Magen stood there gazing at his dream in a sort of ecstatic reverie, his hands gently touching the model, almost caressing it as though it were Michelangelo's *Pieta,* or a beautiful woman.

"Where it is going to be?" I asked.

"What?" Konrad Magen came out of his trance and gave me a startled look, as though surprised anyone was there. "Oh, it's being worked out. You have no idea what it takes. . . ."

He went back behind his desk, suddenly drawing himself back inside his persona as hard-charging real estate tycoon. He gave me a quizzical look, a chilling, penetrating look even, and it was as though he suddenly had fixed me into context.

"What can I do for the *Daily Press*?" he asked pleasantly.

"It's about one of your salesmen. James Kelly."

Magen reacted cautiously, cocking his head slightly and staring at me fixedly for a moment. It was obvious he knew what had happened.

"Oh," he finally said. "Well . . . I saw something in the paper."

"I was wondering if you could tell me anything about him, since he worked here."

"He wasn't one of my salesmen, you know," Magen said quickly, studying me.

"He wasn't?"

"Not for some months, no."

"But he worked here?"

"Yes. Briefly. I filled in the police as much as I could."

"Detective Messina?"

"I don't recall the officer's name. Messina . . . that sounds right. I couldn't tell him much."

"You wouldn't happen to know why anyone would want to kill Kelly?"

"Good heavens, no."

"Can you tell me anything about him?" I went on.

"Such as what?" He was puzzled.

I had to admit I didn't know.

"Did anything happen while he was here that was . . ."

" . . . was what?"

"Well . . . unusual?"

Konrad Magen leaned across his desk. "You're not going to put us in any story about this?" He was alarmed, all right.

"I don't know yet."

"But, surely, just because he worked here briefly doesn't justify dragging us into it. What does this have to do with Magen & Burke?"

I had to admit I didn't know that, either. "How long did he work here?"

"Well . . . " Magen pushed a button on a telephone complex on his desk and spoke into it. "Kerry . . . would you come in, please."

He picked up a Flair pen and sucked on the end of it, watching me. "You read about these things, you know, but . . . " He shrugged.

Then the door to his office opened, and in swept a vision that put my heart into my mouth. A white Celtic face, closely sculpted black hair, an artistically decorated mouth, and green eyes as deep as the Irish Sea off the Cliffs of Moher.

"Mr. Fitzgerald, this is Kerry Burke, my executive secretary."

Kerry Burke walked over and smiled, and I toppled off the cliff.

I had seen her before. James Kelly's lace-curtain girlfriend who used to sit in the back at Kelly's, with her legs agonizingly visible under the table.

"Hello, Mr. Fitzgerald," she said, and it was Gaelic music.

"Hi," I stammered.

"Kerry, how long did James Kelly work here?"

"James?" she said, and her inky eyelashes fluttered. "Let me see . . . I'll have to check that for you."

Magen leaned back in his chair again. "Mr. Fitzgerald is from the *Daily Press*. He wondered if we knew any reason for . . . what happened."

"Oh," said Kerry, and her already pale face went even whiter. She looked down at the floor, as though hoping the awful reality could be avoided.

Was she James's girlfriend? I found myself wondering.

"I really don't know how I could help," Kerry was saying softly. "I told the police all I know."

"Sure."

"I'll check on James," she said, and hurried out of the office on unsteady legs.

Magen shook his head sympathetically. "It was pretty terrible around here yesterday when we got the word," he said.

"Did Kerry know James well?" I tried.

"I don't know," he said hesitantly. "He wasn't here long."

"How did he do while he was here?"

"Well." Magen put the tips of his fingers together and stared at them. "He did some business for us."

"Was he making a lot of money?"

Magen smiled. "That's relative, isn't it? He saw some money."

"I understand he bought an expensive apartment and a car," I said.

"I wouldn't know," said Magen.

"Why did he leave, do you know?"

That was something he could help me with, Magen said. James had left to go into his father's business.

"His bar?"

"I think that's what it was."

I sat there thinking it over. It still didn't make sense.

Then Kerry Burke came back in, carrying a brown folder. She took out a yellow lined sheet with writing on it. "Let's see . . . James was with us for three months. He left last June," she said. "Three months ago, about."

I glanced at her and she was avoiding my eyes, being careful not to make eye contact.

6

KERRY BURKE'S IRISH SEA eyes stayed with me as I walked out of Magen & Burke, rode down in the elevator, through the Kublai Kahn lobby, and to my car on Sixth Avenue. I couldn't get over the feeling that Kerry had to know something about James. I had seen her at Kelly's with James, and I had to think that James had been under her spell. I couldn't blame him there. And that non-look she had given me. What could that mean?

But there was nothing substantial in any of it. The only thing I had found out was that James hadn't worked there. Or at any rate, he hadn't gone back to work there after leaving Kelly's. James's leaving his big job to go to Kelly's had been the slimmest of leads anyway, and now even that was gone.

I drove downtown, deciding to put it out of my mind and get on with the romance of buildings. For a couple of hours, I strolled around inside the great hall at the Chamber of Commerce Building at 65 Liberty Street, off lower Broadway.

It turned out to be a wonderful old place, with a fine, wide Doge's Palace stairway leading up inside it to a great hall the size of a gymnasium, rising two stories high inside. The walls were covered with large, gilt-framed portraits of New York City officials going all the way back to colonial days when they wore satin knickers and powdered perukes. The great hall *was* a lot more romantic than the Nineteenth Precinct, I had to admit.

There on the wall stood an avuncular, gently smiling George Washington, gazing down upon me with green eyes that were trying to avoid my glance. I shook my head and moved on to Alexander Hamilton. But why was his white powdered wig suddenly black, sculpted hair? And why were his eyes, too, dancing emeralds, feathered with dark eyelashes on a Celtic cheek?

I left, and took in the Woolworth Building across from City Hall. The Woolworth had been our first real skyscraper, and has as many lovely curlicues as a French chateau. Then I drove up to Twenty-third Street at Madison Square and looked at the Flatiron Building, which came before the Woolworth Building. It wasn't that they aren't quite fascinating in their own way. They are. But I kept thinking of other structures, the Magen Building, for instance.

That's the trouble with a murder story. It won't let you alone. You keep trying to figure out what could have happened, to arrange some logical sequence of events. With James, it was all a scattered, collapsed pile of rubble. If I could only reassemble those chipped slivers into some kind of a whole, a building of my own.

Okay. James works at Magen & Burke, where he no doubt discovered Kerry Burke. He worked there briefly, Magen had said, and then quit to take over Kelly's, a place for which he had shown nothing but contempt. Then he leaves Kelly's, and a couple months later somebody kills him.

Nothing. There wasn't enough there to even dig an excavation, much less upon which to build a foundation. I began to work up explanations in my mind to tell Timmy why I had to drop the story.

"See, Timmy, I've been assigned to write a series about skyscrapers," I would tell him.

"Skyscrapers?" Timmy's glance would be questioning.

"They're the true signature of the Big Apple, Timmy. . . . "

And there would be Timmy's forlorn face, staring at me with intolerable disappointment.

That night was James's wake out in Bay Ridge. I wanted to go to it about as much as Marcus Aurelius had wanted to fight the Sarmatians. But I went.

Timmy went through it like a sleepwalker, and his wife, Edna, was even worse. She turned out to be an invalid, as I had suspected. In a wheelchair.

"Fitz, this is my wife, Edna," Timmy said at the funeral home after walking me over to her wheelchair. Mrs. Kelly was white-haired, pale as white plaster, and so wasted and frail she was hardly there. Cancer, I guessed.

"Mr. Fitzgerald?" she said in a faint voice. She looked at me as through a pool of water, blinking steadily. "Timmy's told me so much about you."

"I wish I knew what to say, Mrs. Kelly."

Her delicate veined hands held mine, her wrists and arms so thin you wondered how they could sustain life.

"It's God's will," she said softly. "The cars are too fast to be safe."

I glanced at Timmy, and his face said, "Be careful." He shook his head somberly. So, she didn't know the truth.

"Yes," I mumbled. "I'm sorry."

Later when Tim took me to a little bar across from the funeral home for a drink, he stood there shaking his head silently.

"She wouldn't be able to take it," he finally told me.

We stood there at the bar, Timmy in a dark suit with a white shirt and a dark tie, looking like a church usher. "She hasn't been near the store in years," he added.

"You told her it was an auto accident?"

He nodded. "She doesn't see well enough to read the

paper, and there's been nothing on TV. I'm not going to tell her if I don't have to.''

I couldn't get over how different Timothy Kelly looked in Bay Ridge. The easy familiarity of the feisty saloon keeper was gone. In Brooklyn, he was a middle-aged church usher with a terminally ill wife. It fastened the burden Timmy had put upon me even more firmly. My speech about dropping the story evaporated.

"I went to that real estate office," I told Timmy. "James hadn't worked there in several months."

Timmy glanced at me, surprised. "He hadn't?"

"That's what they said."

Timmy reached into his jacket pocket and brought out an envelope upon which he had scribbled something.

"I wanted to show you this," he said, laying it on the bar in front of us. "I talked to that detective."

"Messina?"

"Yeah, that's him. We opened James's safety deposit box today."

"Find anything?"

"Oh, yes," Timmy said eagerly, and smoothed out the envelope. "Look at this here, now."

I looked at the envelope. There Timmy had written, "$350,000."

"What's that?" I asked.

"That's what James had put into his bank account."

I did a double take at the figures. "He had 350 grand?"

"Yes, sir," said Timmy. "I told you he had a big job."

I whistled. "Where'd he get it, did Messina say?"

"Well, no," said Timmy. "But it had to come from that firm. I knew he was doing well. He was buying things like Lord Boycott. A new sports car. That co-op of his."

I lit a Tiparillo and sipped my beer. Magen had been evasive about how much money James had made there.

Of course, I hadn't pressed him, either, since he had told me James only worked there a short time.

"What do you make of it?" I asked him.

"Robbery," declared Timmy promptly. "Somebody knew he had a lot of money."

"Could be," I agreed.

We went back to the wake after that, and a long, somber night it was. Relatives and friends stood about whispering among themselves, smoking, catching up on each other's lives. The funeral parlor was stuffy, heavy with the scent of flowers and that awful, dead smell, and it all continued for a million years.

When I got home that night, I was unable to sleep. Every time I started to drift off, I would come awake with a jerk and see the portrait of George Washington on the wall smiling down at me and saying, "350 big ones."

7

I walked into the *Daily Press* city room the next morning feeling pretty low from the ordeal of the night before, and I still hadn't the faintest idea of how to help Timmy find his son's killer.

I had just opened my coffee container and taken a sip when I realized Ironhead was standing beside me.

"Well?" he said. "How's it going?"

"Not so good," I said, shaking my head. "It's a depressing thing, you know, all those people standing around whispering."

"Whispering?"

"Have you ever noticed that people always whisper around the dead?"

"There was somebody dead at the Chamber of Commerce Building?"

"Oh, that! No, no. Except on the walls, of course."

"There are dead people on the walls?"

"Well, sure. George Washington. Mayors, governors, judges. It's a helluva place, all right."

"What was that about a dead person?"

"Oh. James Kelly. I went to his wake. Depressing."

Ironhead paused to relight his soggy cigar, and to fix me with a look of frustration.

"Will you forget about that murder and get on with the series?" he snapped. "Can you use the Chamber of Commerce Building?"

"Well, it's only about four stories high."

"What?"

"Not part of the skyline."

"Listen," Ironhead declared, revving up, "I don't care if it's part of the skyline! I want an angle! Houseman wants a fill-in on how we're coming along."

"Okay. You can tell him I'm right on top of it."

"And give that murder to Dubbs," he said, stalking back to his desk.

I want you to know that I really was going to call Dubbs Brewer at the police bureau and have him check things out. But I made one last call to Detective Messina at the Nineteenth to ask him about that $350,000 in James's bank account.

"Who told you about that?" Messina complained.

"Sources," I managed to say.

"*Sources?*" Messina harumphed. "You mean his father. Now, listen, I don't want that printed."

"Come on, Messina. A murdered man has 350 grand? How can I not print it?"

"I'm still looking into that," Messina argued. "I don't know what part, if any, it plays in this. Besides, I've got a better story for you."

"Oh, yeah? What?"

"I'll trade you the story . . . if you drop the business about that money."

"How do I know it's good enough?"

"Oh, it is. We got James Kelly's killer."

That stopped me, all right. "Really?"

Yep, said Messina, the case was all wrapped up.

"We got lucky," he said, suddenly in an expansive, talkative mood. Detectives are like that. They don't want you to write about a case while they're still working on it, but once they get a suspect in custody they're willing to tell you what they can, and are not against having their picture in the paper. The police brass notice such things.

"So what's the story?" I asked Messina.

"His bookie got him," said the detective.

"Bookie?"

"Yeah. It seems your friend James was a high roller, and he laid a big bet on his bookie and then couldn't come up with the dough."

"Well, I'll be damned."

"Yeah. We brought the guy in this morning, and we're charging him with murder two."

"Can we get a picture?"

Messina said he and his partner would be walking the suspect out of the Nineteenth Precinct in an hour to take him downtown to Central Booking at Police Headquarters.

I yelled over to Pete on the Photo Assignment Desk to alert him, and then went back to Messina. It turned out that James was a high roller, indeed. He had put down $1,500 on the Yankees against the Boston Red Sox, and the Bronx Bombers had bombed out. When the bookie came around to collect, James couldn't pay, and so the bookie shot him three times.

I'm not much of a gambler, myself. Bike O'Malley once told me that the dreadful trinity of temptations that afficts a man are women, drink, and gambling. "A man can perhaps manage two of them, Fitz," Bike told me sadly from the depths of his own personal experience. "But no man can handle all three." I felt smugly pleased at Bike's profound observation, since the most I usually bet was an occasional dollar on the lottery. But then it occurred to me that I had not always been able to manage even the other two distractions efficiently.

"Isn't that a lot to put on one game?" I asked Messina.

"For you or me, it might be. Not for a high roller."

Some people think the bookie business dried up with the coming of legal Off-Track Betting to New York. Not so. In the first place, OTB only takes bets on horse racing, while a bookie will handle your wager on base-ball, football, boxing, and maybe whether it will rain tomorrow. In the second place, OTB does a strictly cash-in-advance trade, which has been known to cramp the style of a guy who wants to bet on Monday but won't be paid until Friday. A bookie will extend credit and charges no taxes, which is why he will always find plenty of action.

James Kelly, high roller. It seemed to fit. He was a man in a hurry, running with a fast crowd but not really able to keep up. I had once known an over-the-counter floor trader in the stock market who was a high roller. Gambling was simply an extension of his business. He was always being offered free junkets to Atlantic City and Las Vegas by the casinos, because he was a fish. Anybody who walks into a gambling casino with a lot of money is a fish. Or, as Damon Runyon once wrote, "All horse players die broke." The trader used to go through terrifying fluctuations, up $200,000 and then down $500,000. I found it all dizzying, and he eventually crashed, as Runyon predicted.

"Is that where James got all that dough?" I asked Messina. But he was still dodging that subject.

"I don't know, Fitzgerald. But have you ever heard of a gambler winning money like that?"

"Who's the bookie?" I asked.

"Let me see," said Messina, ruffling papers. "Thomas Stern, male, white, forty-two, lives down on Allen Street. They call him Skates."

I typed the notes as Messina gave it to me over the phone, and the little ordinary murder story was getting better. The $1,500 bet was what a city editor would call a good angle, and a murder by a bookie named Skates was pretty good, too.

"How'd you get him?" I asked.

Messina explained that when Skates was in the apartment with James trying to collect, somebody telephoned James. "She was on the phone and heard the shots fired," he said.

"It was a woman?"

"Did I say that?"

"Yeah. You said 'she.' What did she tell you?"

"She just said she was on the phone with Kelly and she heard him mention somebody named Skates."

"Why is he called Skates, do you know?"

Messina muttered something. "No."

"Okay. What else did she say?"

"She heard Kelly say, 'I haven't got the money to pay you,' and then she heard shots."

"How many?"

"Three."

"Who's the woman?"

There was a pause. "Sorry, Fitzgerald. I can't tell you that."

Well, well. So the story also had a female "mystery witness." Even better.

"Can you tell me anything about her? Was she James's girlfriend?"

"Sorry. She called and tipped us to the whole thing, and I promised her confidentiality. You'll find out at the trial."

"The trial?" I wasn't too happy about that. The trial could be a year away.

"What about the gun?"

"Nine millimeter, as I thought. We recovered it"

"Where?"

Silence.

But still, I had a story that Ironhead wouldn't turn up his nose at, and that hopefully would give Timmy the small satisfaction of learning what had happened.

So the cops had gotten Skates Stern in the usual way.

Somebody had dropped a dime on him, which as I said now costs a quarter.

You might have seen the story in the *Daily Press* the next day. Corky Richards got a photo of Skates Stern as he was being led out of the Nineteenth between Messina and his partner, a white-shield cop named Maloney.

Skates fitted my idea of what a bookie should look like, all right. He was short and round, wearing a camel's-hair sport coat, a polo shirt open at the neck, and a straw fedora with a garish scrambled eggs band around it. He looked out of the photo in the paper with wide, darting, crazy eyes. He seemed totally indignant.

8

AND THAT WAS pretty much the end of the James Kelly story, I thought. Timmy called me with fulsome congratulations, even though I hadn't actually done much.

"Well, at least it's over, Fitz, and I owe you one," he said.

Ironhead was pleased, as well. "Now you can put your mind on the series," he said pointedly.

"Yeah."

"When you decide which buildings you want to use, tell Pete on the assignment desk so he can get photos."

"Okay," I said, not too happily.

Being rid of the James Kelly story was a mixed blessing, that was obvious. The damned buildings of Manhattan once more loomed over me in all their obnoxious and varied splendor. Where the hell to start when there was such an embarrassment of riches?

The World Trade Center, with its infinity of glass walls climbing to Mount Olympus? Well, it would be nice to go up to the Windows on the World on top and contemplate the city while having a Shaefers, that was true. Rockefeller Center? The Metropolitan Life Building with its Jello-colored space capsule on top?

I was still running them through my mind when the phone rang, and there was a wild, raving maniac on the line.

"Is that you, Fitzgerald?" the voice shrieked.

"What . . . who's this?"

"It's Skates Stern! What the hell you doin' to me? That story's crazy! I gotta talk to you."

"Stern?" I asked, trying to get my bearings. "The guy who shot James Kelly?"

"Ahhhhhheaaa!" The voice went into cardiac arrest. "I never shot nobody! Get outa here!"

"Where are you?"

"Where the hell ya think—in the goddamned Tombs!"

"What do you want from me?"

"I want you to come down here and talk to me! This whole thing's all balled up."

When you work for a newspaper, you get some rather unusual calls and letters, including some from Rikers Island or Dannemora. A reporter doesn't make a habit of dealing at length with such communications because the caller or writer is always a convict who believes himself to be Alfred Dreyfus or the Man in the Iron Mask. Inmates at the Tombs, which is the Men's House of Detention attached to the grimy Manhattan Criminal Court Building at 100 Centre Street in lower Manhattan, are allowed two phone calls a day. Skates had used one of them to call me.

"You want an interview?" I asked Skates, intrigued a little in spite of myself.

"I wanta set you straight," he railed.

I drove down the FDR Drive in my tilted Mustang, parked behind Police Headquarters, and walked up to the Tombs, wondering what Skates Stern wanted to tell me. You go in through an iron door on White Street, and then through an iron gate. Only after that iron gate is closed are you allowed through another iron gate into a sort of lobby. On the other side of the lobby is another iron gate that lets you into the Tombs itself.

A correction officer led me down a hallway into a large, airy room filled with wooden tables and benches, and there I found Skates chain-smoking at a table, his eyes flitting about like an eagle's. He half-rose when I approached him, and waved his hand.

"Fitzgerald?" he asked anxiously.

"Yeah." I sat down across from him.

Right away, Skates Stern started talking to me as though he had known me all his life, and his tone was that of an old friend who had been basely betrayed.

"Jeez, that was some job you did on me in the paper," he complained, leaning across to stare at me. "What'd I ever do to you? Huh? Where'd you get all that crazy stuff?"

"What crazy stuff?"

Skates was digging into three different pockets to find a pack of cigarettes and then a match. All the time he was talking.

"What crazy stuff? Whata ya mean, what crazy stuff!" He found his cigarettes. "That Mickey Mouse you put in the paper!" He found his matches. "Where do I get off shooting a fish like Mr. Kelly?" He lit up.

"You didn't shoot him?"

"How?" he whined. "With a ballpoint pen?"

"Detective Messina said a nine millimeter automatic."

Skates wagged his head around, looking at all four walls and the ceiling as though searching for help from the air. Finally he came back to me.

"How can I shoot anybody which I never fired a gun in my life! What am I, bald-ass loony?"

"I don't know what you are, Skates. I write what the cops tell me."

"The cops say I shot the guy cause he wouldn't pay off a bet?"

"That's right. They said you were James's bookie."

"Okay, so I'm a bookie! So what? What'm I gonna be, a goddamned astronaut, comin' outa Brooklyn? But am I stupid too?"

"I only know what the police told me, Skates."

48

The short, round bookie leaned across the table, his eyes dancing wildly. With his straw fedora gone, you could see he was almost bald. "Did the cops tell you they wanta indict me for murder? Huh? Me? Skates Stern who would'n' hurt a cockaroach?"

I noticed that Skates's normal conversation was to talk in questions, and scrambled ones at that.

I looked the little punk over, waiting for some whining excuse. Whatever it was would be totally lost on me. "What do you want from me?" I asked him.

"I want you to get me outa here!"

"Me?"

"I don't know who else to ask."

"You'd better understand me, Skates," I told him. "The way it looks from here is you killed James, and he's the son of a good friend of mine. I'm not interested in helping you."

Skates didn't even blink. "Put me away! Go on! Lock me up like a frozen mackerel in the deep freeze! Shoot me, give me the chair, inject me with cyanide! But tell me what I done first! Tell me how I done it! Tell me and I'll jump outa the window, you won't havta push!"

I let his excited words rush over me, and then said calmly, "Just keep in mind that I'm a reporter."

Oh, he knew that, he said. Hadn't I murdalized him in the paper and got him locked so deep inside the Tombs it would take the USS *Iowa*'s guns to blast him back out?

"Well, remember that anything you tell me could end up in the paper," I told him.

"Jeez! Now *you're* readin' me my rights!"

"I'm not—"

"It's okay . . . I *want* it inna paper! It's the only chance I got, because all the DA says is I done it. Mr. Fitzgerald, wring my neck like a turkey, I didn't do it! You gotta get me outa here. I'm countin' on you."

Well, that was certainly lovely. Timmy Kelly was

counting on me to get Skates put away forever, and Skates was counting on me to get him out. How do I inspire these baseless hopes in people? It's because I'm a reporter, and people don't realize how disorganized and powerless we really are. I tried to think, while Skates hunched over the table staring at me anxiously.

"Look, Skates, I didn't put you in here. The murder did."

"Which I don't know nothing about, on my mother's head!"

"Have you talked to a lawyer?" I finally hedged.

"Lawyer . . . *lawyer*? You mean a Legal Aid kid that's about twenty-one? All he wants to know is what do I wanna plead guilty to?"

"Can you hire another one?"

"With what? Who am I, Barbara Radziwiller?"

The conversation was getting out of hand. Here I was talking to the man accused of killing my friend's son, and somehow he expected me to help him.

I leaned back and lit a Tiparillo. There was sort of desperate sincerity in the roly-poly little guy, it seemed to me. Naturally, the Manhattan District Attorney was seeking a murder indictment against him. That was the charge.

"Now, listen, Skates, Detective Messina says you shot James with a nine millimeter automatic, and he's got the gun."

"Sure he's got the gun! He got it from my desk drawer which I don't know how it got there. I got it for Mr. Kelly because he says he's walking around with lots of bread. Which he is, because he always pays me cash."

"What?"

"Sure! He's got the money stuffed in every pocket."

"No, no, the gun. You say you got it for James?"

"Yeah! I tell Squeaky Duffy this guy needs a piece, see, and—"

"Wait a minute, Skates." I was trying to keep his machine-gun story straight. "You bought the gun that killed James?"

Skates shoved himself around and made a face like somebody who can't stand it. He wagged his head, put his hands over his eyes, and then stared fixedly at me.

"Jeez," he finally said. "Listen, will ya? If you're gonna help me, ya gotta get this straight."

"If *I'm* going to—"

Skates laid his hands flat on the table. "I bought the piece for Mr. Kelly. It was *his!* I don't know from any damned guns. Then they bust me for what I don't even know, and this dick with the crooked nose says he finds the gun in my desk at Walsh's which it hadda be planted there."

My head was spinning. Skates was sitting there convicting himself, and I was in a dither.

"Were you at James's apartment that night?"

"Sure! I go up there, he pays me fifteen hundred he owes me, and I leave."

"He *paid* you?"

"Sure! He always paid me in cash! Almost always bets long shots, always loses! Nicest fish I ever met. Am I gonna shoot the goose who's giving me golden eggs alla time! Gimme a break."

I was feeling more and more uncomfortable, talking to the bouncy Skates Stern. You can tell when a guy is spilling his guts without trying to hide a thing. Skates spouted his answers nonstop. A liar goes a lot slower.

"What about the phone call?"

"I hadda call you at the paper . . . what else could I do?"

"No, no. The phone call to James when he was shot."

"Phone call?" Skates pondered, searching his memory. "Oh, yeah, somebody called while I was there."

"Skates, that person heard James say he didn't have

the money to pay the bet, and then she heard you shoot him three times."

Skates Stern's head sank onto the table in slow motion, facedown. He stared into the wood for a full second. Then he looked up at me, forlorn.

"Mr. Fitzgerald, put an ice pick through me! Nobody said nothing about not paying. Nobody shot nobody! I got my dough and left."

I sat there studying the excitable little man, and his story was worth about four cents wholesale. But I was still listening.

I found myself wishing I'd never come to the Tombs.

"Tell me about the gun," I said.

Skates rattled off his account of the gun deal. James had told him he needed protection because he carried a lot of money. So Skates had talked to his pal Squeaky Duffy at Walsh's down on Allen Street and had gotten the gun.

"Squeaky says the heat's on so bad he's gotta have twenty-five hundred, which I paid him and gave the gun to James. That's all I know about it till that crooked-nose cop sticks it up my grumper."

"Naturally, there was no gun permit," I put in.

"Gun permit?" asked Skates, baffled.

"Okay."

"So ya see, I'm innocent!"

I had to marvel at Skates Stern. Innocent? He had just admitted to a felony in buying an unlicensed gun, not to mention being a bookie, which is also illegal.

"Come on, everybody's got guns!" he replied unruffled.

I studied Skates Stern, who was watching me eagerly. "So you bought the gun that killed James," I said. "You were at his apartment the night he was killed, and they find the gun in your desk. But you didn't do it."

"To put it precisely—exactly!"

"Then who did?"

"Who am I, Columbo? I don't know. Ask Squeaky. He sold me the gun. He's got a desk next to mine at Walsh's. After the murder, the gun winds up in my desk, next to his. He's got to be in on this."

"Tell me about Squeaky Duffy," I said, not sure I really wanted to know.

Duffy, Skates explained, is a guy who has a desk next to his in the back at Walsh's, and who is in the "six-for-five" business, meaning he's a small-fry loan shark. Duffy also sold people things they couldn't buy at Macy's, such as illegal handguns.

"He also sells stuff that falls offa trucks, ya know? Sometimes the stuff gets some help falling off."

"You think Duffy got James?"

"I don't know. He knew James had lots of scratch because I told him, with my big mouth," Skates mourned. "And he was mad at me because I gave him an inside tip one time and it didn't pan out. He keeps asking me for his money back, 'cause Duffy only deals in sure things."

"Have you told the cops about all this?" I asked.

"Cops?" Skates's mouth went into a prune. "Every time I tell them something, they say they're gonna use it against me."

"So the cops haven't talked to Duffy yet?"

"I don't know," said Skates. "I kept callin' Walsh's and Duffy's never there."

I told Skates I still didn't see what I could do.

"Go talk to Duffy!" he pleaded.

"If he was in on it, why would he talk to me?"

Skates lit another cigarette and thought that over. "Yeah." Then he got another idea. "Look, talk to Jerry . . . slip him some dough."

"Jerry?"

"The bartender. Give him a hundred."

Here was somebody else who thought reporters walked around with fat rolls.

"Why should I?"

"Because you got me in here!"

I sighed but let that pass. "Where do I get the hundred?"

Skates glanced around, as though to make sure nobody was listening. "Okay. I got a room upstairs over Walsh's, see? In the refrigerator, under the ice cube trays, I got a stash. Take a hundred for Jerry."

It was a fine mess, all right. I was slipping idiotically into helping Skates Stern, which would outrage Ironhead Matthews, since I would be shooting down my own story. It would infuriate Detective Messina, who had an air-tight case. And what would Timmy Kelly say?

But Skates's anxious tale held me like the Ancient Mariner's glittery eye held the wedding guest. Because, with everything stacked against him, my instincts were telling me I believed him. Only a desperate bookie would tell a stranger where his "stash" was. Ordinary murder was turning into a can of wriggling worms.

9

ALLEN STREET IS in the Lower East Side, a continuation of First Avenue when you get below Houston Street. It's down there by Orchard Street and Ludlow in a very old neighborhood where they still have a public bath and an outdoor market. These old neighborhoods are forever being squeezed in from all sides with warehouses and housing projects. But there are still second-hand clothing stores and hardware stores and slanty old saloons with neon "Miller Light" signs in the windows. The old *New York Journal-American* was down at the foot of Allen Street on South Street, and now the *New York Post* is in the same building.

I found Walsh's between Delancey and Canal Street, a grimy, old, wooden shanty of a bar jammed between a plumbing supply house and a second-hand store. A warped, wooden door with chipped paint next to the bar let me into a dark hallway, and I went up the steps to the second floor. There was Skates's room, a number six written on it in pencil. I let myself in with the key he had given me.

Racing forms and betting slips and tout sheets were scattered all over a round table in the center of the room. Stacks of paper everywhere, and across one wall three TV sets, one of them an impressive-looking cable hook-up that must have been tuned constantly to the race results. In a cramped little kitchen, I found the refrigerator, and inside the freezer, rolled up in an old woolen sock, I found Skates's frozen stash. Looked like quite a roll. I took a frozen hundred dollar bill from it and put the rest back. Apparently the money he had collected from James.

Back down the wooden steps and outside, and then into Walsh's. Inside, there was a long, scarred, wooden bar with big, smoky plate-glass mirrors on the wall behind it, the edges beveled to form clear frames. You had the feeling it had been there since the days of Tammany Hall. In the back were bumper pool tables, a couple of video games, and two scarred, wooden desks.

There were a couple of men in shabby clothes drinking beer from glasses at the bar, and the bartender sat near the front hunched over the *Daily Press*. I slid onto a bar stool halfway toward the back.

"Yeah?" the bartender said, glancing up. He was pudgy with a pale, indoor skin and wore a blue dress shirt with no tie.

"Whatever you got on draft," I told him.

The bartender put his newspaper aside, walked to the center of the long bar, and drew me a glass of beer. He put it in front of me.

Being Irish and a newspaperman, people sometimes take me for a cop at first glance. Sometimes it helps, sometimes it doesn't. At the moment, sitting there in Walsh's, a stranger in a local bar, it didn't.

"Jerry?" I asked.

He cocked his head and gave me a closer look.

"Skates Stern sent me."

"Oh, yeah?" Jerry the bartender said, shaking his head. "Jeez, that's tough. You his lawyer?"

I almost smiled. So I was being upgraded. Since he seemed willing to talk to me, I let him think what he wanted for the moment.

"Skates is in deep shit," I told him.

"Yeah, I saw it in the paper." Jerry was quite edgy

56

talking to me, an unknown quantity in his little bar. I glanced toward the back, but there was nobody at either of the desks.

"Which desk is Skates's?" I asked.

"The one on the right."

"The other is Squeaky Duffy's?"

Jerry sort of nodded, and mumbled, "Uh, huh. He ain't here. Ain't been around lately."

"So I heard."

"I don't know anything," Jerry offered. "I'm just the bartender, you know?"

"Were the cops in here?"

Were they in there? Oh, they were in there, all right, Jerry said. "All over the place!"

"They found the gun in Skates's desk?"

"Yeah. Jesus!"

"Anything else?"

"I don't know. Like what?"

"Well, did they question you?"

Did they question him! Jerry let fly a mournful litany of anguish. Here was Jerry Shapiro, a working man, a taxpayer, an honest bartender, treated like a member of La Cosa Nostra. Just because he picked up a lousy $25 apiece from Skates and Squeaky Duffy for renting them desks, he was supposed to be a goddam crime czar!

"I told them I didn't do nothing," he concluded.

"Did they talk to Duffy?" I asked.

"See, he's been out-a-town," said Jerry.

"Do you know where?"

"Brooklyn."

"Brooklyn?"

"That's where he lives. By Flatbush Avenue."

"Did the cops go out there, do you know?"

"I don't know nothing, mister."

I sighed and lit a Tiparillo. "Well, did the cops ask about Duffy?"

"All they cared about was *me* and what's a gun doing in my place," he complained indignantly.

"What Skates wants to know is how the gun got into his desk."

"How'm I supposed to know?" Jerry wailed. "I just rent them those desks, that's it."

I asked him if he had seen anybody other than Squeaky Duffy hanging around in the back around the desks.

Well, Walsh's wasn't the Waldorf-Astoria, and there was no doorman, and they didn't have a Kennedy airport metal detector, said Jerry. And in fact a stream of basically undesirable types came and went all the time, including gamblers, hookers, pimps, deadbeats, shoplifters, muggers, drunks, and horseplayers.

"Which any of them can't be trusted," he concluded.

"So you're telling me anybody could have walked in and put the gun in his desk?"

"Yeah, I guess so."

I put the hundred dollar bill on the bar. "Skates thought you could tell me where to find Squeaky Duffy."

Jerry eyed the bill and blinked. Great decision-making machinery revolved inside his head. Greed was at war with caution.

"How do I know you're his lawyer?" he wanted to know.

"I'm not his lawyer."

Jerry wavered unhappily. "I already told the cops everything."

"Jerry, I'm not a cop. I'm a reporter. Fitzgerald, *Daily Press*."

Jerry sort of waved his hand at the *Daily Press* he had been reading. "Yeah, I saw your story."

"Listen, Jerry," I told him, "nobody's going to drag you into this. I just need to find Duffy."

Somebody walked into Walsh's just then, and went along the bar, behind me, and into the back. Something

58

flitted across Jerry's eyes, and he reached out and took the hundred.

I glanced into the back. The man who had come in was sitting at Squeaky Duffy's desk.

10

THE MAN AT the desk in the back was watching my every move. He had some papers out on the desk in front of him, and a pen poised in his hand, but his eyes were on me. I got up and carried my glass of beer back to his desk. I sat down. Squeaky Duffy hadn't moved, except for his eyes being glued onto me.

"Yeah?"

"Duffy?"

"Who wants ta know?"

"Skates sent me. He's in trouble."

Squeaky Duffy finally lowered his hand that held the pen. He sat back a little. Duffy was all caution. His hair was black and combed back slickly over his head, and he wore a blue sport jacket that clashed with his brown trousers. But he had a tie on.

"Yeah, I heard about that," Duffy finally said. "Who're you?"

"A friend," I said, and paused to light a Tiparillo. It gave me time to notice Duffy's evasive mouth and the bunched muscles around his eyes as he squinted at me. It gave Duffy time to size me up, too.

"You a dick?"

"Newspaperman. Ed Fitzgerald, *Daily Press*."

Duffy's alert eyes narrowed. He didn't seem to like that any more than if I had been a detective.

"I don't know nothin'."

"Now, listen, Duffy. I'm not here to break your shoes. All I want to know is if you sold Skates a gun."

A deeply hurt expression of innocence and amazement swept over Squeaky Duffy's face.

"A gun?"

I puffed on my Tiparillo. Squeaky Duffy wasn't going to give me the time of day. I wasn't too surprised.

"Skates told you I sold him a gun? Jeezus Christ!" He shook his head as though plainly astounded. But I saw some fright there, too.

"Did he say he wanted it for somebody else?"

"I don't know nothin' about no gun," Duffy pleaded, and I heard a curious sort of squeak coming from his throat.

"Have the cops talked to you yet?"

Squeaky Duffy mounted to the Cross before my eyes. Spears jabbed him, and a crown of thorns was placed upon his entirely blameless head. Why would New York's Finest possibly want to talk to him? The mere suggestion was offensive, terrifying, and unmentionable.

"They got Skates for murder, Duffy," I told him. "That gun killed somebody, so they're going to come looking for you, too. So you might as well tell me."

"Did Skates tell the cops I sold him a gun?" Squeaky asked anxiously. Squeaks emanated between every word.

"I don't think so. He wanted to find out if you were going to help him first."

"How can I help him when I don't know about no gun!"

I watched his quivering, evasive mouth and heard his stuttered protestations, and I knew that what Skates had told me was true. I got up, said "Okay," and looked at a little desk against the wall across from him.

"This is Skates's desk?"

He looked around. "Yeah."

"The cops found the gun in this desk, did you know that?"

Squeaky looked away. "Yeah, I heard. That's tough. I been out of town. I was outa town during this whole thing. I just got back. I may have to go away again."

"Sure," I said. "Did you ever see anybody around this desk?"

"Who?"

"I don't know. Anybody."

"Well, jeez, anybody could walk in."

Duffy was nervous and didn't like my questions. He pretended to think deeply.

"People come in, I don't always know who they are."

"What kind of people?"

"All kinds. Gamblers to see Skates. Some fancy hookers sometimes. Like that."

"Skates thinks you planted the gun in his desk."

Squeaky's face went into a swoon. "What? Did Skates tell the cops that?"

I watched him for a moment to let him simmer. "Skates hasn't told the cops anything—yet. He's looking for help first from his friends."

Squeaky drew back, as though removing himself from that suddenly dangerous connection.

"Why would I plant a gun on Skates?" he asked me urgently. "Especially if it's a gun I sold—which I didn't. Do I want cops down here on me?"

"Well, then, who planted it here?"

Squeaky sat back and tried to think, making his nervous rat sounds.

"Did you ever see a stranger in here by his desk?" I asked. "Somebody you hadn't seen before and maybe never saw again?"

Squeaky made a face and wanted me gone. "I don't know," he moaned. "The only strangers came in are people who are lost or maybe their car broke down, like that woman.''

''What woman?''

''Her car broke down and she had to come in and call Triple A or something. She sat at the end of the bar and had a drink while she waited.''

''Did you see her near the desk?''

''No. Well, just when she wrote down a number.''

''She *was* at the desk?''

''She looked up a phone number, you know, and then sat at Skates's desk to write it down.''

''When was that?''

''Just before we heard this guy was shot.''

''Will you tell that to Detective Messina?''

Squeaky turned away and rubbed his face. ''What for? What good would it do?''

''Will you tell the cops the whole thing? Selling the gun to Skates, too?''

The loan shark's voice rose into one sustained squeal.

''I don't know nothing about no gun!''

I could see that Skates's chances of being helped out of his jam by Duffy were about a million-to-one. Duffy had troubles of his own.

11

THAT AFTERNOON I went back to the office and wrote a story that made me feel like a loathsome double agent. Not that it wasn't rather colorful, since it was about Skates, but I knew it would make Timmy unhappy. That's the trouble with a story. It doesn't always go the way you expected, or might have hoped.

I dropped in a little about Squeaky Duffy, too, but didn't use his name. Actually, I *couldn't* use his name because even though I didn't believe Duffy's denials about selling the gun, still it was possible that it was true. And the last thing I needed was a libel suit on a story that Ironhead didn't even want.

Fortunately, Ironhead was busy on a cop-murder that day and didn't have time to harass me.

I sent the story to Jim Owens, the assistant city editor, and had to hope that he'd find space for it, and that it might spook Duffy into talking.

After work I walked down Third Avenue with Bike O'Malley, who used to ride a motorcycle until he somehow went off a pier into the Hudson River.

I guess I was still feeling uncertain about Skates because I asked him, "Know anything about bookies?"

"They are to be avoided at all costs," declared Bike, who did not always practice what he preached.

We went into Kelly's, and Timmy spotted me at once. He came right over to me. "Hi, Fitz," he said. "Anything new?"

I sat there feeling like a traitor. When Timmy saw my latest story, he would be unhappy. I had to try to explain what was happening.

I was all prepared to bare my breast of my nefarious doings, until I looked into Timmy's eager face.

"What's the matter, don't I even get a drink?" I stalled.

"Sure. All you want. On the house," Timmy bubbled, which didn't improve my churning guilty insides much.

"That bookie called me," I plunged in.

The red-faced bar owner bummed one of my Tiparillos. "He did, did he?" he said. "What did the murderin' bastard want?"

I sipped the stein of Harp beer Timmy had put in front of me. "I went down to the Tombs and talked to him."

Timmy leaned across the bar, all ears. "You did, did you? Did he tell you why he did it, the bloody savage?"

It was impossible. How could I tell him that I still wanted to help find out who killed James and why, but that now I believed it had not been Skates Stern?

"Well, Timmy," I replied evasively, "he said James had made a lot of bets with him, and that James had a lot of money."

"Sure. We knew that. He was doing good at that real estate place."

"That bothers me," I told Timmy. "All that money."

"Why?"

"If he was making all that dough, why'd he quit to come down here and run your place?"

It was easily explained, said Timmy. That had been just a job. But Kelly's was his heritage. Of course he would come down and take over the family business.

"Did you ever find out how James made that money? Did he make a big sale, do you know?"

"Well, now, Fitz, he never told me much about his uptown doings, you know? But I guess he must have."

The more free steins of Harp beer Timmy shoved at me, the worse I felt.

There I sat, Benedict Arnold being treated by George Washington, and too cowardly to even tell Timmy the truth. I guess I should have just refused the free drinks, but the fact is the more I thought about it the more beers I seemed to need.

Another free Harp, and I slid into self-disgust.

Another, and I realized a beautiful wench named Wanda was sitting beside me, smiling at me openly. Did I wish to buy her a drink? Nothing would please me more. It would help me stop thinking of the mess I was in. As we know, beauty is in the eye of the beholder, and when the beholder has had enough steins of Harp beer, beauty is well-nigh universal in an available woman sitting beside you howling with abandon at your slightest witticism.

"You wanta go out?" she finally suggested.

"Hmmm?"

"I can make you real happy," she cooed with what I suddenly realized was professional familiarity.

"You in business?" I asked, rather startled.

"Sure," she smiled. "You've got enough on the bar for me, honey."

The beautiful in my-Harp-beer-eyes wench picked up my money on the bar, stood up, took my arm as though to lead me out of Kelly's, and the floor collapsed beneath me.

The collapsing floor took the form of a very large man who stood up next to the hooker, pulled out a gold shield, and announced he was a vice squad detective from the Public Morals Squad, and that he was busting the hooker for soliciting.

"What . . .?"

Timmy galloped down behind the bar to find out why the woman was screeching like the wheels on an A Train rounding a curve, and why I was standing there looking like somebody had hit me with a ball peen hammer.

"What the hell's going on?" Timmy demanded.

The morals squad detective flashed his gold shield again and said he was taking the hooker in.

"I don't allow hookers in here!" Timmy protested.

"Yeah?" the cop said sarcastically. "Well, what do you think this broad is, a social worker?"

"Take your hands off me, you hump!" screamed Wanda the non-social worker.

"Wait a minute," I finally managed.

"Forget it, Mac," the cop said. "I saw you give her money, and I heard it all. Let's go, sweetheart."

"Okay, okay," Wanda said, "so I'm a hooker! So you got me! I been busted by better creeps than you!"

"Yeah, yeah, yeah," said the cop, and led her out.

I sat there stunned. What a day this had been. What a rare mood I was in. Why, it was almost like being run over by a taxi.

12

AFTER THE COP dragged the hooker out of Kelly's, Timmy stood behind the bar looking like someone who had just gotten an electric shock treatment.

"Where the hell'd she come from?" he finally asked me, speaking from a basement.

"I don't know. All of a sudden she was sitting beside me," I mumbled.

"Jesus!"

It's the worst kind of bad news for a bar owner to have a hooker arrested in his place. Any kind of an arrest for illegal activity in a bar is bad news—gambling, serving minors, fights, allowing hookers to work out of the place. These things are reported to the State Liquor Authority and can lead to suspensions of the bar license, or even revocation. Which is why Timmy stood there looking like a ghost.

"What happened?" he finally managed.

"Timmy, I was just sitting there, and all of a sudden she's coming on to me."

Bike O'Malley stood there frowning, wagging his head sagely. "Fitz, you should have realized."

"Why?"

"A good-looking broad like that, and she's making up to a hump like you? There's gotta be something funny."

"Thanks a lot."

Timmy slugged down a shot of Irish whiskey, something he almost never does while working, and stared disconsolately at the bar. It was a wonderful end to a wonderful day for me. I had turned traitor on him, and now I was putting his license in danger.

I slunk out of Kelly's and went up to my place on East Eighty-second Street, looking for a place to hide. I made some corned beef hash and eggs and tuned in to the New York Mets baseball game on TV.

I couldn't concentrate on the game, though. The hooker bust and the James thing were both running around inside my mind. It wasn't Keith Hernandez out there at Shea Stadium fighting the dastardly Chicago Cubs. It was Squeaky Duffy and Skates Stern. And sitting in the stands behind home plate was James Kelly, his pockets stuffed with cash, betting on the outcome. With him, urging him on, was Wanda the hooker.

The only way I could block out Wanda was by thinking of James's murder, and I didn't know what the hell to think about that.

Actually, it was only then that it began to sink in. If I believed Skates Stern, then the whole damned James murder was wide open again. If Skates hadn't done it, then who had? If what Skates told me was true, then he was only a pawn in this thing, a rather shady one to be sure. So who was the chess player who had used him?

Squeaky Duffy?

It was certainly possible. If Duffy knew James had lots of money, he would be capable of going to James's apartment to get it. Or sending one of those assistants of his who help things fall off trucks. But Duffy's plaintive cry floated into my head. "Why would I want to bring cops down here?" I couldn't answer that one.

Was Squeaky another pawn, also pretty shady? Okay. Queens pawn opening. Duffy hears from Skates that James Kelly has money stuffed in every pocket. He either goes to see James or sends a truck hijacker to steal it. He gets James's money. Then he hides the murder weapon in a desk right next to him. Idiotic.

But if Skates and Duffy were both pawns, then who were the other knights and rooks in this game? And who was the chess player moving them around? And of course, I realized there was another pawn in this game now. Me. By talking to Duffy, I had placed myself on the board.

I wasn't particularly on Skates's side. But James Kelly wasn't coming off as a completely innocent dupe, either. Sometimes it isn't entirely clear who has clean hands in a murder case.

The umpire suddenly looked out of the TV set at me and called time. "What did James want with that gun?" the umpire asked me. "Where'd he get all that money?"

I snapped off the set, but the questions didn't stop. If Skates bought that nine millimeter automatic for James, how did it come about that somebody killed James with the same gun? And who was that on the phone who told Messina she heard shots fired, when Skates said there were no shots? Somebody was lying.

I gave up and retreated to the bathtub, my refuge from the world and its annoying problems. I slid down into the water and picked up my copy of *Meditations,* the wisdom of the ancient Roman emperor Marcus Aurelius, to whom I sometimes turned for inspiration.

"A spider is proud when it has caught a fly; so is a man when he has caught a hare, another when he has taken a fish in a net, another when he has killed wild boars or bears, another when he has captured Sarmatians," declared Marcus to me. "Are they not all brigands, if you look into their principles?"

"All brigands." Marcus was including himself, of course, because he was fighting the Sarmatians at the time he wrote that. And Marcus was right, of course. People act in their own self-interest. The spider does not examine his principles from the point of view of the fly. Timmy wanted Skates hanged, no matter what. Skates got James a gun as a service to a free-spending fish. Squeaky Duffy sold guns without troubling himself about how they might be used. The witness on the phone said she heard shots fired. Was she mistaken, or was there some self-interest there, too?

That umpire stopping the Mets game to harangue me made it clear that I was entangled in the damned case again. Or still. If Skates had told me the truth, the whole scenario collapsed.

"*Nobody said nothing about not paying,*" Skates had moaned. "*Nobody shot nobody! I got my dough and left.*"

And yet, Messina had told me that a woman had been on the phone with James and had heard him say he couldn't pay. And then she had heard shots.

A dictum floated into my head. *Cherchez la femme.* Follow the woman. I realized I had to find that woman who had nailed Skates, the "mystery witness" I'd written about.

And by now, I had a pretty good idea who that witness had to be. A white Celtic face with nervous, black eyelashes fluttering on her cheek as she looked away from me, and eyes as green as the Irish Sea off the Cliffs of Moher.

13

BEFORE I COULD even have a cup of coffee the next morning, the phone was ringing. I slopped out of the shower in my bathrobe and picked it up, water still dripping from my hair.

"What is this crap?"

"What?"

"What the hell's the matter with you!"

The sledgehammer on the other end had an angry voice and a bent nose. Detective Messina. My story about Skates in the *Daily Press* had clearly ruined his breakfast, and now he was going to ruin mine.

"What're you doing, Fitzgerald, turning this bum into a choirboy? I thought James Kelly was your friend."

"Yeah, well . . ."

"Yeah, well *nothing!*" Messina wasn't interested in listening. He was interested in chewing me out. "We nail this skel for you, and now you write him up like he was an altar boy."

I was going to explain that Skates Stern was probably Jewish, but it seemed irrelevant.

"Dammit, Messina, I talked to Skates, and—"

"And he played a violin through the whole thing! Who told you to talk to a defendant? Who do you think you are?"

It was a fair question. Who did I think I was? An ink-stained wretch caught in the middle.

"You believe this guy?" Messina wanted to know.

72

"Well, Messina, I guess I do."

"Why, for God's sake?"

"I don't know. He sounded sincere."

"A sincere bookie?" Messina was disgusted.

It was a phrase right out of "Fugue for Tinhorns" in *Guys and Dolls,* and I felt myself wavering.

"Do me a favor," the detective went on. "Check with me the next time you're about to do a swan dive off the board, huh? I might be able to tell you if there's water in the pool."

"Anything new on the case?" I asked hopefully.

"Sure there's something new," he came right back. "You don't think I called just to chew you out, do you? That's a waste of time."

"What happened? A new suspect?"

"No! We've got the suspect. Thomas J. Skates Stern! We don't need any other suspect, will you get that through your head."

"So what's new then?"

"Your pal Skates has just been indicted." I could imagine Messina's face. The cat that ate the canary.

"I didn't say he's my pal, Messina. I just think you've got the wrong guy."

"Let me worry about that."

"But if Skates didn't do it, the guy who did is still out there," I protested.

"Nobody's still out there." Messina was final. "It's all over. The case is cleaned up. I've got no more time to spend on it, you understand?"

Oh, I understood, all right. Homicide detectives have so many murders stacked up that they can't spend forever on one, especially an ordinary one. If it's the Bernhard Goetz case, that's different, that's priority because the public can't get enough of it. You've probably heard about the Goetz case. He shot four kids who he said tried to mug him on the IRT subway. But in the

James Kelly murder, Messina had a good suspect, and he wasn't about to look for any more. I understood. I even sympathized with Messina, but I couldn't drop it; not just yet.

"But what about all that money James had?"

"What about it?"

"Where'd he get it?"

"From selling real estate. It's got nothing to do with this."

Wonderful. A guys who runs around saying, "Tennis, anyone?" has $350,000 and then gets killed, but it doesn't have anything to do with anything.

"Did he make it at Magen & Burke?" I asked.

"Make what?"

"The money."

"Will you forget about the money!" snapped Messina. "What are you trying to do, make Kelly a suspect here? He's the goddam victim!"

"Messina, look, I'm not trying to screw up your detail, but the only way I can chase a story is to follow my nose."

"And a goddamned big one it is, too!"

I couldn't think of an answer to that.

"Now, who is this guy you said sold Skates the gun?"

"What?"

"You said in your story somebody sold Skates the gun."

"I thought you didn't believe Skates."

"I don't. But maybe the guy can help us."

So, there it was. They would get Squeaky Duffy and turn him into a prosecution witness, which would be easy to do. Instead of helping Skates, Duffy would drive the last nail into his coffin. Duffy would deny selling Skates the gun and testify to anything to save his skin, and Skates's last hope would be gone.

"Listen, how about a trade?" I suggested.

"What?"

"Sure, like the other time when I didn't print anything about the 350 grand. I'll tell you who the guy is if you'll tell me who that witness is."

"Witness?"

"The one who said she heard Skates shoot James."

"Cut the crap, Fitzgerald!"

Messina was getting annoyed. Cops are not interested in bargaining with reporters, and have the idea you're supposed to be tickled pink with whatever scraps they're willing to let drop.

"Are you gonna tell me the guy's name, or should I call the district attorney and ask him to persuade you?" He was annoyed, all right.

"You've already got him indicted," I parried. "What harm would it do now to talk to that witness? What's the big problem?"

Maybe if I could talk to the witness before the cops got to Duffy, I could write a story that might flush Duffy out to help Skates.

Messina was off on a tirade, however.

"Because she talked to us in confidence, goddammit! Because I promised her anonymity until the proper time. Because she's my chief witness and I don't want her hassled! Because I don't have to tell you *anything!* Do you know what obstruction of justice means?"

The big guns were being cranked into place, I could see that.

"But, Messina, Skates says there were no shots fired. He says he was paid and left. I saw the money."

"What?" Messina's voice rose. "Where is it?"

Why had I blurted that out?

"If you know where evidence is, you'd better tell me while you still can."

"Dammit, if Skates had the money James paid him for a bet, then how could he kill James for not paying him?"

"I'll figure that out. He probably robbed him."

"Then how could that woman have heard James say he couldn't pay?"

A sort of muffled, jagged blur of rage blasted through the phone. Messina was sick and tired of my meddling and idiotic questions. He was not going to be cross-examined by a goddam nosy buttinski reporter! Withholding evidence was a dangerous game, and how would the *Daily Press* like to know about that?

Visions of sour-faced Charles W. Corcoran, the newspaper lawyer, leaped into my head. Not to mention a scowling flame-thrower known as Ironhead Matthews. And behind him stood a befuddled John McFadden, our publisher, wondering why I was even bothering with the story when I was supposed to be examining the architectural flowering of the Big Apple.

But there's a stubborn Irish streak in me, too, and I don't like to be threatened and bullyragged any more than the next guy. Because I was getting annoyed, too.

All Detective Messina wanted to do was build a case against Skates Stern, which is his job, of course. But I was interested in following the story wherever it led.

"All I want is to talk to that witness," I tried. "Skates said—"

"Skates said . . . Skates said . . . goddamit, if Skates told you he was about to be canonized by the pope, you'd believe him!"

I gathered he wasn't going to help me.

"Listen, forget it," he snapped. "We'll find this guy ourselves. But your office is going to hear about this! You goddam reporters aren't above the law!"

Bang! Errrrrrrrr. Silence.

Wonderful.

With that lovely beginning to the day behind me, I made some coffee and read my story at the table in the kitchenette. It seemed mild enough to me. Then the phone started ringing again. Who would it be this time? Had Messina already called the *Daily Press* and sicked Charles W. Corcoran on me? I didn't answer it.

It was time to talk with Kerry Burke—she had to be the witness—if she were willing to see me. I called the real estate office and was put through to her.

"Hello?"

With a rush, the delectable image of Kerry invaded me. I saw the Celtic face, the haunting eyes, and the tantalizing figure that made me weak.

"This is Ed Fitzgerald, *Daily Press*."

"Oh, hello! I was just thinking about you!"

Oh, God, what little things can make the day of an ink-stained wretch. The glorious Kerry was thinking about *me?*

"That's nice," I managed.

"Yes," she went on cheerfully, "did you hear the news?"

"What news?"

"They indicted that man! It's such a relief, I can't tell you."

"Listen, I was wondering if we could talk."

"Sure," she bubbled brightly.

"Where can you meet me?"

"Do you want to stop by the office?"

"No, somewhere else."

"Ohhh. Well . . . let's see . . . there's a place around on Fifty-sixth where I stop for coffee sometimes in the morning. Madame Charriere's, it's called."

"Fifteen . . . twenty minutes?" I asked.

"See you!" she breathed, and it hit me like an immense neon sign in Las Vegas flashing a welcome.

14

I PUT IN A quick call to the *Daily Press* and asked Glenn, the switchboard guy, to tell Ironhead I'd be a little late.

"You want Ironhead?" he asked.

"No, just tell him." I didn't want to give Ironhead a chance to tell me to forget it. "Corcoran hasn't been looking for me, has he?"

"No. Why?"

"Nothing."

I got dressed and drove up to Madame Charriere's, which turned out to be a little yellow French tea shop designed to look like something in St. Germain des Pres in the Left Bank students' quarter in Paris. I walked in and didn't have to look twice to find Kerry Burke. I immediately spotted the Celtic face, the black hair styled closely around her head, the green Irish Sea eyes at a little table just inside.

Her smile lighted up Madame Charriere's as I crossed to her table by the window and sat down. She was drinking tea, so I ordered some, too. It came in a tasteful brown pot.

She gazed at me eagerly, a very different person from the wary creature I had first met at Magen & Burke.

"Well," I said, "you're certainly looking chipper."

She laughed a little and lit a cigarette. "I'm just so relieved that it's all over," she sighed.

"Messina called you?" I asked.

She nodded pertly. "This morning! I guess it's not something to be happy about, when you think of what happened, but . . ."

"You're the witness, aren't you?" I said, trying to keep my voice level. But she still gave me a startled look, and her face flushed.

She sipped her tea and didn't say anything. It was as good as an outright admission.

"It's all right. I know all about it."

"What . . . how?"

"I'm a reporter," I said, using a dodge that usually works.

"Oh." It worked, all right.

"You're not going to put me in the paper, are you?" Concern in those green eyes.

"Not if you don't want me to. Not if you'll talk to me."

"Well, I don't mind talking to you," she said, giving me a dazzling smile. "I mean, as long as they've got him. But if you put my name in the paper I'll be in trouble, won't I? They told me not to discuss it."

Vulnerable, wide-eyed innocent sitting there wondering what I was trying to get her to say. It was time to do some bluffing and quiet her fears.

"Now, look, Kerry, I pretty much know the whole thing already."

"You do? Well then . . .?"

"I want to be sure I'm right, and I need more details."

"But . . ." There was still the anxiety of a good citizen on her face, and a little fright at being exposed as an informant.

"You don't have to say a word," I went on.

"I don't?"

"No. I'll talk, and if I'm right you don't have to say anything." It was a device used by reporters, sometimes, with an informant who wants to be able to say truthfully that he didn't open his mouth.

"You were on the phone with James when he was killed?" I said, and her eyes flashed affirmatively. "You heard him mention Skates Stern's name, and say he couldn't pay the bet." Another eye contact agreed, so far.

"Then you heard three shots fired?"

A nod of her head. She couldn't stay with absolute non-movement.

"Did you ever meet this bookie?" I asked.

Kerry puffed on her cigarette and couldn't keep from talking any more, which is what I had hoped.

She exhaled smoke. "I think I met him once in the Monkey Bar," she said.

"The what?"

"It's a bar in the Elysee Hotel. He stopped by our table one time."

"Did you ever hear James make a bet with Skates?"

"Yes."

"Often?"

"He bet a lot."

I twirled the teaspoon in my cup. "Did he usually win?"

"He must have won sometimes," she smiled. "He certainly had money to spend."

I looked at her again and started in. "After you heard the shots, you called the police and told them about it," I said, and she watched without contradicting me.

"Then Detective Messina brought you in, took you before a grand jury, and you testified," I continued. "Then they indicted Skates."

Kerry was nodding her head again. "I'm just glad it's all over," she said.

"You'll have to testify in open court at the trial," I told her.

Kerry flushed at that. "But they told me he'd probably plead guilty, and I wouldn't have to."

"Who told you that?"

"Detective Messina."

Wonderful, I thought. Messina was going to tie up Skates so tight he'd be willing to save the state the expense of a trial.

"I wouldn't count on that," I told her.

"Why not?"

"Because I don't think Skates is going to plead guilty to anything."

"They told me it was practically open and shut," she said, some of her sparkle diminishing.

"It opened okay, but I don't know how easily it's going to shut," I told her. "There are some problems."

"Such as?"

"For instance, if James had as much money as everybody says he had, why would he tell Skates he couldn't pay a bet?"

Kerry pondered that. She shrugged. "Maybe he didn't think he owed it?"

"Maybe. But I also can't understand why Skates would shoot him. Then he'd never collect. Are you sure the noises you heard were shots?"

"Yes."

"Are you sure you heard him say 'Skates'?"

"Yes, Mr. Fitzgerald." A flinty, challenging glare. "Do you think I imagined it?"

I backed off. "No, I'm sure you heard what you heard."

"Well, then . . .?"

"Do you believe in instinct?"

"In what?"

"You know, you have a feeling—"

"A *feeling*?"

"Skates is no killer."

"And how do you know that?" she snapped irritably.

"I talked to him in the Tombs."

"You did?"

"And the business about the gun. Killed with his own gun. Skates couldn't take a gun away from a school crossing guard."

Kerry was looking pale and puzzled. "How do you know it was James's own gun?"

"Skates told me."

"You seem to put a lot of credence in him," she sniffed.

That stopped me. Skates's persuasive line of gab sounded in my head. Then Messina's sneer came to me. "If Skates told you he was going to be canonized by the pope, you'd believe him."

"Maybe it'll make more sense after the cops talk to Squeaky Duffy," I said, thinking aloud.

"Who?"

"This guy Skates says sold him the gun."

Kerry was in a dither by now. "You know who sold Skates the gun?"

"Yeah. This guy down on Allen Street. The cops haven't found him yet, but they will."

"And you still think Skates is not involved?"

"Oh, he's in it up to his chin, all right. But if Squeaky backs him up, he might have a chance. I think Squeaky saw who planted that gun in Skates's desk."

"I don't understand you," she said suddenly, leaning over the table. "I thought you were James's friend."

"Well . . . his father's."

"And here you're trying to help the man who killed him?"

"Not exactly. . . ."

"Well, *I* was James's friend, and I'm not interested in helping his killer . . . or you!"

"Wait a minute, Kerry . . ."

"They've got the man," she declared angrily. "James called me, and I heard it all! It's over . . . finished! I'm not going to be dragged through any more of this."

I thought she was going to cry, but there was sterner stuff in her than at first seemed to be the case. The almost-tears changed into a glare of challenge.

"Were you James's girlfriend?" I said, trying a new tack.

She looked into her tea and frowned a little. "We went out a few times. It wasn't serious. Not with me, anyway. Why?"

"Because it won't help James to pin this on somebody who didn't do it."

The glare returned. "What makes you think he didn't do it, other than *instinct?*" She did a pretty good job of contemptuously mangling *instinct*.

"It just doesn't add up," I said rather lamely.

"What doesn't?"

"None of it. James making all that money and then leaving to run a bar."

"What does money have to do with it?"

"Kerry, it usually has plenty to do with things. Did he make $350,000 at Magen & Burke?"

"What?" Kerry was livid now. "Are you trying to drag *us* into this?"

"Us? Who's us?"

"Magen & Burke. I work there too, you know."

"Magen & Burke," I mused, only now making the connection. "Are you *the* Burke?"

"My father was a partner before he died. I'm afraid he rather made a mess of things. But Mr. Magen gave me a job and has been wonderful to me. So—"

So don't ask for help that might hurt her boss, she was probably going to say.

"I'm just trying to find out something about that

money James made," I tried again. "Do you know anything about it?"

Kerry's earlier, open cheerfulness had retreated into that same, nervous defensiveness I had noticed the first time I had met her. She was definitely on her guard now.

"I don't know all the details," she finally said.

"Could you find out for me?"

Kerry's eyes opened wider, as though she was suddenly identifying me as the enemy. "You probably should ask Mr. Magen these things."

That wonderful, immense neon welcome sign was flickering.

"I have to be going," she said, snuffing out her cigarette. The neon sign flickered faintly and went out.

I stood up. "I didn't mean to upset you," I mumbled. "If I find out anything more, I'll call you again."

Kerry seemed to freeze. She glared at me. "Call me again? What for? I've told you all I know. I cooperated with the police." She snapped her purse shut, and her face was tight with anguish. "I never should have gotten involved in this," she declared.

"But you are," I said. "Involved, I mean. You're the only real witness at the moment."

Kerry was a stone statue. "Well, I'm not going to do it!" she said, white and trembling. "This is the last time I talk to anybody!"

"What!?"

"There, are you happy now? Your precious bookie is off the hook, as far as I'm concerned. You tell that policeman to leave me alone!"

"What do you mean?"

"I mean forget it!" She turned and hurried out of the cafe. There was nothing I could do, really. She strode past the outside tables and off toward Sixth Avenue. I couldn't really blame her for not wanting to be dragged into it.

I sat there staring into my tea, and suddenly realized what I had done. I had just gotten rid of Detective Messina's only witness. Now I would find out what trouble really was. I felt like an idiot. I had been had by Skates Stern. I was a gullible patsy, after all, and it was now clear to me that I was halfway off the diving board, and what I was looking down at was concrete.

15

I DROVE DOWNTOWN to the office after leaving the yellow teahouse, and had that feeling that a storm was beginning to build around me. My bright idea to *cherchez la femme* had only succeeded in getting *la femme* furious with me. And Messina might be calling the *Daily Press* to complain, too. And in spite of all that, I didn't feel I had gotten anywhere.

I walked into the city room to my desk, sat down, lit a Tiparillo, and tried to figure out some other tack. It occurred to me that there might be a better guide than *cherchez la femme,* and that might be *cherchez l'argent.*

Follow the money.

Except that Magen hadn't told me very much, and Kerry was too sly to be tricked into spilling it.

A twisted face, scrunched into a lopsided winking came to my attention. Bike O'Malley sat across from me going through facial contortions to call my attention to something behind me.

"What?"

A warning whisper. "The smoking lamp is lit."

I glanced around, and there sat Ironhead at his desk, puffing on his cigar, staring a hole into my back. When he finally had my eye, he glanced darkly up at the four-sided newsroom clock over the city desk, his subtle way of asking why I had come in late.

I walked over to him and sat down.

"Well," he grumped, beslobbering his cigar and glaring at me as though I were a mugger in a lineup, "I see you still haven't mastered the intricacies of the simple, modern device known as the alarm clock."

"I can explain . . ."

"Oh, I'm sure you can," he snapped irascibly. "You're good at explanations. Your car broke down again, right? Where the hell do you buy these goddam junkers, Fitz, at a Bronx auction?"

"The car's fine," I said.

"Well, then, I suppose you fell asleep in the john at Costello's again, and they closed the place up on you, and you were forced to sit there all night swilling booze until they opened up this morning?"

"That was Bike O'Malley, Ironhead."

"If you don't mind my asking, how are we doing?" he asked.

"Well," I said, "I talked to Kerry Burke, but she either doesn't know much or won't tell me much. She's the mystery witness."

That seemed to distract him a little. "Mystery witness?" City editors love mystery witnesses, especially if they're beautiful women. "What'd she say?"

"Not a lot, but maybe enough to keep the story alive."

A tug of war was going on inside Ironhead's percolating skull. I knew he would always prefer a good story to a crazy series, but there was the problem of Mr. McFadden.

"Have you at least gotten started on the series?" he frowned.

"Sure. I looked at the Flatiron Building."

Ironhead allowed himself to hope. "And . . . ?"

"It's nice."

". . . *nice* . . . ?"

"And I looked at the Woolworth Building, too."

"Yes . . . ?"

"It has gargoyles on it."

Ironhead made a face not unlike one of the gargoyles and spat something revolting.

"All right, do the damned interview. But it better be good."

I went over to Glenn the switchboard guy and asked if there were any messages for me.

"Listen," I said to Glenn, "didn't you tell Ironhead I was going to be late?"

"Uh . . ." Glenn mumbled hazily. "Oh, yeah . . . I got the message right here." He handed me a slip of paper.

"Didn't you give it to Ironhead?"

"Well, it's here in his message file."

Wonderful. Newspapers are in the communication business, but it's always a gamble trying to get a message to anybody or from anybody. We write on sophisticated, electronic televised screens, and the circuitry and printing are all Star Wars systems. But trying to get a message to anybody in the city room is like sending up smoke signals.

I went back to my desk and wrote a story about Skates Stern being indicted in James Kelly's murder, and then put in some of the interview with Kerry. I didn't use her name, though. I didn't want to cause her any more grief. There wasn't any way I could bring in the $350,000, which frustrated the hell out of me.

How to find out about that money? I needed somebody at Magen & Burke who would talk to me. But who?

"Magen & Burke," came the mellifluous voice of the vinyl-covered receptionist.

"Yes, ma'am, I'm trying to reach one of your salesmen, but I've somehow misplaced his card."

"I see. Well . . . would you like to speak to Mr. Magen? Who shall I say is calling?"

"That's all right. The salesman showed me a building, and I want to make sure he gets the commission. Who handles building sales?"

"Well . . ." She apparently was consulting a list. "Could it have been Mr. Dragget?"

"He's a friend of James Kelly's," I offered.

"Oh." A pause. "Well." Another pause. "Uh . . . Archer Whitney, perhaps."

"Yes," I said. "That's the one. Could you connect me?"

Things went click and bleep, and in a moment Archer Whitney came on the line.

"Whitney here."

"Hello. This is Ed Fitzgerald, a friend of James Kelly's."

Archer Whitney drew a blank for a second. "Yes?"

"Maybe you heard what happened to him?"

"Yeah," said Whitney. "Too bad."

"I'd like to talk to somebody up there who knew him."

"I guess I knew him," he said laconically.

"Very well?"

He chuckled a little. "I could write a book."

"Could I buy you a drink?" I offered.

"How about lunch?" he came right back. Apparently I had found one of those "uptown" types Timmy always boasted about. A drink wasn't enough. Had to be lunch.

"Okay," I said. "Any place in particular?"

"How about Turley's . . . on Sixth Avenue?"

I told Ironhead I was going out to look at some buildings.

"Don't get lost," he flung at me.

I drove across Forty-second Street and north up Sixth Avenue to Turley's, near Radio City Music Hall and the Rockefeller Center complex, where NBC types hang out.

Whitney had said he would be waiting at the end of the bar, and I had no trouble spotting him. A gray suit and a striped tie and styled, uptown hair. A regular thirty-year-old Yuppie. He was drinking a martini on the rocks.

"Whitney?" I said, walking up.

"Ah, yes," he smiled, and gave me a quick once-over. Of course, I'm not a Yuppie, but there seems to be a sort of recognizable patina about a newspaperman that shows. Anyway, he picked it up right away.

"Drink?" he asked, and "Beer," I replied.

"You look like a reporter," he said.

"Thanks . . . I guess. I am. *Daily Press*. You look like a Yalie."

Archer Whitney laughed and gulped his silver bullet. "Close. Amherst."

"Don't they call that the little Ivy League?"

"Sometimes. So what happened to Bjorn?"

"Who?"

Whitney smiled. "That's what we used to call Jimmy. Proud of his tennis, you know."

Yes, I remembered Timmy had said something about that. Bjorn Borg, the Swedish tennis star.

"Well, I'll tell you, Whitney, somebody shot him. As you probably know. And I'm trying to find out who, what, when, where, why, and how. Like a reporter."

"Aha," he said, and sipped again. "Jimmy was a piece of work, all right."

"Were you a close friend?"

Whitney grunted contemptuously. "Huhhh!" I got the impression he wasn't.

"No, huh?" I tried again.

"He didn't really have any close friends, as far as I knew. He was suspicious. Didn't think people really liked him. I think it was because he didn't make D.U."

"D.U.?"

"Delta Upsilon. He wanted to be a D.U. a whole lot. They're pretty big at Amherst."

A fraternity. It squared with the impressions I had of James. Things like that mattered to him. He had a desperate need to be accepted by the Sulka tie world, for some reason. It wasn't easy for me to quite understand

90

such things because my father was a teamster and I never had any doubts about who I was. "Stay with the guys that brung you," my father used to tell me.

The picture of James that was emerging was that of an outsider and a loner, a kid with his nose pushed up against the window at the candy store and finding no welcome.

"How did he come to join Magen & Burke?" I asked.

Whitney sort of sneered. "He looked up Kerry, I guess, and she took him to Magen."

"Kerry Burke?"

He gave me a surprised look. "You know her?"

"I talked to her the other day. We had tea."

"*Tea?*"

"Yeah. I was asking her about James. Were they an item—Kerry and James?"

Whitney's face got red and he gave me a scornful look. "What? For chrissake."

"He was taking her out, wasn't he?"

"Yeah, he was spending money on her like an Arab sheik. But she laughed at him. She wouldn't go for a phony like that. I've known her for years . . . I used to go with her when she was at Smith. We were sort of engaged."

I looked at the Waspy Whitney in his striped tie and realized why he hadn't liked James. Whitney's torch for Kerry Burke burned brightly, and it was obvious he couldn't stand the attentions toward her of a pushy saloon-keeper's son from Brooklyn who hadn't even made D.U.

"So you were all three close when you were at college?"

Whitney shuffled his feet and put his other foot on the bar rail. He didn't seem to like the characterization.

"Not close. Kerry and I were going together, and he sort of hung around . . . like a fifth wheel."

Eventually, the ivy-covered days at Amherst and Smith had ended, and Kerry and Whitney both wound up at Magen & Burke. Glancing at Archer, I had to think it hadn't been a coincidence on his part. And then one day James had also shown up.

"That's when James and Kerry started dating?" I asked.

"They weren't . . . *dating*," Whitney muttered.

"Well, she went out with him, didn't she?"

A pained face. A grudging admission. "Yeah. He followed her around like a St. Bernard. Maybe she felt sorry for him. It was embarrassing. Hell, he couldn't get to first base." He chuckled happily at the memory.

Sometimes when a person hates somebody, you can get things out of that person that they might not tell you otherwise. I felt Archer Whitney could tell me a lot, so I rubbed more salt into his passion wound.

"But he apparently did," I coaxed him.

He nodded sourly. "I don't know how, except that he spent money on her like water. Things have been kind of tough for Kerry since her father died, you know. She likes a good time."

"You mean he bought her?"

"What?" he snapped, and there was a hard glint in his eye. "What the hell's that mean?"

"I only mean that he put a rush on her with money."

Whitney calmed down a little. "Yeah. Somehow, he hit it big. I don't know how."

"When did that happen?"

"I don't know, exactly. A few months ago he seemed to have stepped in clover. That's when he put the big rush on Kerry and bought an apartment in her building."

"What?"

"Sure. I told you he was a damned bloodhound. He moved in one floor beneath her. She was disgusted."

"Kerry told you that?"

"Sure. But she couldn't do anything about it."

So, all of a sudden, James Kelly had come into a lot of money.

"I understand he was a high roller," I said. "Maybe he made a big score on a bet?"

Whitney laughed. "Come on! He lost constantly. Bjorn never played the odds, always the long shots. Hopeless. He must have gotten it from his father the barkeep."

I already knew that was nonsense. If it hadn't come from gambling and it hadn't come from Timmy, there was only one other possibility.

"How was he doing at Magen & Burke?" I asked.

Whitney gave me a quizzical, sidelong glance. "Good question."

"So what's the answer?"

Whitney drained his martini and ordered another. I kept waiting for him to get us a table.

"I understand he made a lot of money," I prompted him.

"Who told you that?"

"I just heard about it," I stalled.

He turned on me. "That's ridiculous. He was pathetic. Practically a gopher." The martini came and Whitney sipped it.

"Magen told me he saw some money."

Whitney gave me a look. "You talked to Konrad Magen?"

"I'm talking to everybody. He said James made some money."

Whitney grunted. "He was always dropping these broad hints, you know? Something very big was always cooking."

"But you don't think anything ever came off?"

"Hell, no. It was all bullshit."

"He didn't sell anything?"

"Hell, no. In fact, I think he screwed the pooch, because they canned him."

"He was fired?"

"Sure. That kind always ends up out the door."

"How long did he work there?"

Whitney rolled his head back. "Not long. Few months, maybe."

"So you don't think he could have made $350,000 working there," I tossed out.

Whitney squared around and gave me a sarcastic look. "Are you kidding? For what?"

"I was hoping you could tell me. He got it somewhere, and I don't think it was from the daily double."

Whitney put his martini glass down on the wooden bar and moved it around, making wet, interlocking rings like the Olympic Games logo. I had gotten his attention, all right.

"You're certain of this?"

"Yep."

"I'll be dipped," he said, but new wheels apparently were beginning to turn.

"Something occurs to you?" I prodded him.

Whitney shook his head, confused but on a scent. "Not exactly. It's just that . . ."

"What?"

"The whole thing about him didn't make sense. I always had the feeling something was going on, but I couldn't figure out what. He was tight with Magen, but I couldn't see why they even hired him. Then he had a lot of money. Then he was gone."

"So you haven't a clue as to how he could have made 350 grand at Magen & Burke?"

Whitney shook his head. "I'd sure like to know," he said.

He had nothing on me. I left him with still another martini. He never did get us a table.

16

I HAD BEEN looking for something unusual in the James Kelly murder. Well, I had found it. Somebody had paid James $350,000, and I couldn't find out what he had done to earn it, or who had paid it to him. Coming out of Turley's I glanced up Sixth Avenue and saw the glass and chrome monolith in which Magen & Burke had their offices. Automatically I headed that way. It was time to ask Konrad Magen, the pseudo NFL cornerback, about that money, because there was no place else it could have come from.

Once again I was shown into Magen's office overlooking midtown Manhattan. Once again I sat on the gray executive couch, lit a Tiparillo, and glanced at the glistening model of the Magen Building. Konrad Magen of the barrel chest and powerful presence sat behind his desk and smiled at me.

"Well," he said expansively, "I see they've arrested the man in James Kelly's murder. If you want a statement from me, you can say we're all very pleased it's been cleared up."

"That's not what I wanted to talk to you about."

"Oh?"

"No. There's another little thing that bothers me."

"What's that?"

"I found out that James deposited $350,000 in his bank account while he was working for you," I said.

"He did?" Magen gave me one of his bland looks.

"Did he make it here?"

Another bland look. But no response. Magen leaned back in his immense leather chair. "I don't quite understand," he said. "Why are you asking me this?"

"Well, if he made that money, I'd like to find out what he did to get it."

Konrad Magen was pensive, then perplexed. Why was I prying into his business?

"The case is closed, Mr. Fitzgerald. They have the man in custody. I gave the police a full account of James's short stay here. If you're writing another story, I don't see the need to mention us."

"I don't like loose ends," I told him. "And 350 grand is a very large loose end."

"You seem to think you're a policeman and that I have to talk to you." That bland look was shading toward stiffness.

"His father's a friend of mine, that's all."

"Well, that's commendable, I'm sure. But I don't want to be mentioned in any story."

"Why?"

"I'm a private businessman," he said, and there was a snap at the end.

"Okay," I said, and made it clear I wasn't satisfied. I got up to leave.

Magen was standing now, and his voice was a little more conciliatory. "Are you going to write this, or is it only for your own information?" he said.

"I don't know yet."

Magen sat down again, and so did I. An absolutely benign Chamber of Commerce expression slid over his tanned face. He wasn't trying to hide anything, but he didn't feel the need to broadcast his business to the world.

"Other people in this office might get upset," he told

me, "if they knew James had made a big commission like that."

"So it did come from you?"

"Yes. He did make one good commission."

I didn't think I heard him correctly.

"Did you say *one* commission?"

"He helped me sell a building, yes."

"James made $350,000 on the sale of *one* building?"

Magen didn't even blink. "Yes."

"What the hell did he sell—Yankee Stadium?"

Magen smiled, and sat there swiveling his high-backed brown leather chair to and fro. "A sizable building in Manhattan."

"What building?"

"Now, I really don't think I have to tell you that." He seemed rather miffed.

I sat there letting it run around in my head.

"I don't get it," I said, thinking aloud.

"What?"

"Why would you fire somebody who made a sale like that?"

"Fired? No, no. He resigned."

You know how it is when somebody smiles calmly at you and says, "The moon is made of green cheese?"

"He quit?"

"Yes."

"Do you know why?"

"Something about going with his father."

Magen still wore his bland smile, but I had out a telescope and was examining the lunar surface for signs of cheese.

James Kelly of the Sulka ties and Amherst dreams walking away from a job that would pay him a $350,000 commission on one deal to take over Timmy's saloon?

Cherchez l'argent was leading in some weird directions.

17

I WAS PAST the chrome-and-vinyl receptionist and the potted plants, going toward the elevator, my head awhirl in the unfamiliar ether of high finance, when she caught up with me. Before I could say a word, the elevator doors opened and she stepped into the car. We started down.

"I'm sorry about this morning," she breathed, standing close enough for me to peer deeply into the Irish Sea and to smell the heady scent of heather.

"I didn't mean to upset you."

"I know," she smiled. "You're just doing your job."

"Did you mean that . . . about not being a witness?"

Kerry shook her head. "No, no. I have to be a witness. I owe James that much."

The elevator doors opened, and we walked out into the immense Kublai Kahn lobby past the fountain. I lingered before going out.

"Buy you a cup of coffee?"

Kerry nodded, smiling a welcome at me. Inky, long eyelashes on a Celtic cheek. The Irish Sea eyes looked at me appealingly, and I was lost in a Gaelic mist. We walked into the coffee shop, a soaring Roman atrium of a place, all glass and Art Deco walls.

Kerry wore a hugging sheath of a shimmering blue dress that showed off her lithe figure stylishly, and very high heels that did the same thing for agonizingly attractive legs.

We sat in a booth, and she lit a cigarette while the coffee came. Slim fingers and a slim white cigarette and a delicate red mouth. My slide continued. I was turning into another St. Bernard.

"I really do want to help," she said softly. "This morning, I don't know . . . you threw so many questions at me, and . . . I thought it was all over. You talked like it was just beginning."

Something had happened, I felt. This was a different Kerry Burke. Apparently she had realized I wasn't an ogre. Maybe some of my questions had bothered her the way they bothered me.

"If there's anything I can do," she said, leaning across the table toward me, holding her coffee cup in those delicate hands, and watching me with those eyes.

Ah, yes, there is Kerry-berry, I was thinking. It might not solve James's murder, but it would greatly improve my ragged bachelor existence. I wish I could tell you that I was a great success with women, being a hotshot *noospaper* reporter and all, but the unhappy fact is that I seem to disappoint women, sooner or later. They all seem to want more of me than I'm able to give. Some want long psychologically revealing conversations, and probe for some sign that you "aren't afraid to show your inner feelings," which seems to mean that you're supposed to have latent feminine characteristics or something, but which always means that you're supposed to defer to them and be something of a wimp. I guess the way I am shows through eventually, and they go looking for somebody who's a better candidate.

"There's a lot you can do," I told her, coming out of my reverie. "I understand James made $350,000 on a deal with Magen & Burke, and I need to know about it."

Kerry's pretty face flushed and she looked away. Then she looked back. "I guess that's what bothers me," she murmured.

"What?"

"Asking questions about Mr. Magen. You mustn't think there's anything . . . improper . . . about that money."

Konrad Magen, she assured me, was a pillar of the real estate business, a man above reproach, and a personal friend who had saved her life by giving her a job after her father had died.

"Daddy left the firm in a mess, but Mr. Magen took me in anyway," she explained.

"What kind of a mess?" I asked.

She shook her head impatiently. "It's not important. The important thing is, Mr. Magen didn't hold it against me. Without him, I don't know . . ."

Looking at her, I had the feeling Kerry had always been used to the best. Konrad Magen, she seemed to suggest, was allowing her to keep living that way.

"Kerry," I told her, "I'm not saying Magen is mixed up in anything. I'm just following my nose. That's the way you chase a story. Your Mr. Magen confirmed that he paid James $350,000, and the next step is to find out what he paid it for. All I need to know is what building James sold."

"Mr. Magen wouldn't tell you?"

"Not specifically."

"Uh-huh." Kerry sat there nodding her head, pursing her lips, thinking. "Well, I can assure you, it's perfectly all right. If it'll make you feel any better, I'll find out about it for you."

"Will you?" I said brightly. "You're wonderful."

Kerry smiled at me. "It looks as though I have to, or I'll never get rid of you."

"Are you trying to?"

Ah, me, how the classic Kerry fielded that hesitantly launched flirtatious dart. A teasing half-smile, a slight tilt of the nose, and a glance from those sun-darting eyes.

"Not really." A smile that lifted me. "In fact, maybe if I help you, you'll think of something else to talk about."

That I would, Kerry. That I would.

"Okay," she said with finality. "To show you that Mr. Magen has nothing to hide, I'll get you the information." She leaned across the table and touched my hand, and a shiver went up my arm all the way up under my scalp. "He just doesn't want the wrong kind of story."

"I understand."

I was quite amazed at the turn of events. Kerry Burke would be my Trojan horse at Magen & Burke?

"I'm also curious about why James would quit," I said. "I thought he'd been fired."

"Fired? Who said that?"

"Archer Whitney."

She looked down into her coffee. "Oh. You've been talking to Archer, too?"

"Oh, yes," I said. I was talking to everybody I could find. I glanced at her. "You have a champion in Whitney."

She blushed. "I know."

Before I could stop myself, I had blurted out something impertinent. "Are you and Arch . . . I mean . . . are you still going with him?"

Again, the female response, the coquette surfacing. The sly smile, amused, toying. I was a transparent puppy trying to clamber into her lap. Kerry Burke was accustomed to the fumbling, fawning half-passes of twitterpated men.

"Arch is very nice."

What a lovely reply! I floated disembodied. Kerry only smiled enigmatically. It was time to reach out and find something to hold onto.

"Arch told me James moved into your building."

Kerry sighed. "Yes. I asked him not to. But . . ."

"Is that how he came to Magen & Burke? You got him a job?"

"I didn't *get* him a job. I introduced him to Mr. Magen."

"Doesn't that seem funny to you? About James?"

"You mean that he looked me up?" A tormentingly deft suggestion that I didn't consider her attractive enough to lure a man?

"No, no," I stammered. "I mean, that he made a big sale and then quit."

Her inky eyelashes fluttered and she turned her head to the side. "Lots of people come and go in real estate," she explained.

I sipped some coffee. "Yes. But not after making a big sale. It doesn't make sense."

"Lots of things don't make sense."

"I know. But in a murder, they have to. If they don't, that's what you look for. All that money, and he quits."

"You think money's behind it?" she asked then.

"It usually is. That's what I'm working on, anyway."

"You're not going to give up, are you?" she said, studying me.

"I can't yet."

"All right. You want to call me later on this afternoon?"

"Count on it."

The delightful little laugh again. "All right. By then I should know what you want."

I think she could probably detect already what I wanted. She could be my Trojan horse and my Celtic inspiration at the same time, as far as I was concerned.

"You won't tell Mr. Magen about anything I tell you?"

"Scout's honor."

She smiled at that, and even laughed a little. "I've never met a reporter before."

That got my attention. Was I a little daffy, or was there

the beginning of a welcome in her eyes and manner? Extremely beautiful women always make me nervous, especially when they reach out to me. I know I'm supposed to look at women, even glorious ones, as just other human beings, but all the persuasive talk in the world can't penetrate to where desire lives.

There was something about Kerry Burke that seemed unreachable, somehow. What was it? I had thought of her as lace-curtain Irish, and maybe that was it, an aristocratic air. Or was it simply the delectable sheen of Smith College? Anyway, I was both intimidated by her patrician manner and madly attracted by her beguiling beauty and the stylish elegance of her. She looked— what?—cultured. And extremely expensive.

"Maybe we could have a drink some time, and I could tell you all about it," I ventured.

Another friendly smile. "That would be nice."

Well, the compass was still spinning. We had just about spun around 180 degrees.

I walked out of the Kublai Kahn lobby in a state of imprisoned rapture. Kerry Burke's performance had absolutely taken me into camp. She could do with me what she wished.

I smiled wistfully at the idea that she was my Trojan horse at Magen & Burke. She was also a Trojan horse who had wiggled inside the walls around an ink-stained wretch. Of course, I had left the gates of Troy wide open.

18

THAT AFTERNOON I called Kerry from the *Daily Press*, and she had the information for me.

"It looks like it was the Bayton Building," she said quietly over the phone.

"Bayton Building? Where is it?"

"Let me see." Papers shuffled. "Over on Broadway north of Columbus Circle . . . 1694 Broadway."

"That's the one James sold?"

"Yes."

"What was the selling price?"

"Uh . . . in the millions . . . I don't know exactly."

"Okay, Kerry. Thanks."

"You won't say where you got this?" she said anxiously. "I don't want—"

"Promise. Nobody will get it out of me even with a thumbscrew."

"I hope I'm doing the right thing."

"You are."

"It's listed right here in the book. I got it from Mr. Magen's office. He was paid for the Bayton deal. Doesn't that clear it up?"

It was hard to quarrel with that. "It seems to."

"*Seems* to?" she laughed.

" . . . well . . ."

"Still running on instinct?"

"I'll call you tomorrow."

An inviting chuckle. "Don't forget."

I hung up and stared at the information. So James had been paid $350,000 for selling the Bayton Building. All right. I pondered it a moment. All right, what? I didn't know. Kerry saw nothing curious about it. Why should I? Except that I didn't believe it. Of course, my disbelief was based on a rock-like foundation of instinct.

Who could I ask about it? Magen? No. He considered it routine. Detective Messina? He didn't seem to think there was anything to it. Timmy Kelly? He thought James could sell fish to Fiji islanders.

And then I got it. The person who shared my disbelief.

The voice coming over the phone was a little slurred, no doubt from that martini lunch at Turley's.

"Whitney?"

"Yeah."

"It's Fitzgerald."

"Ah, yes, the inquiring reporter."

"Arch, I found out what James sold to get that commission."

A grunt. "Huh! He didn't sell a birdhouse."

"It was the Bayton Building above Columbus Circle."

There was a silence. Then a sarcastic, "What?"

"Yes. You know anything about that?"

Whitney sort of laughed. "I know all about it. I got the lead on that deal first."

"You handled the sale?"

No, Whitney conceded, he had been "screwed out of it" by Konrad Magen, "which isn't unusual."

"So why couldn't James have sold it, then?" I asked.

Whitney grunted sarcastically. "Because he didn't even have a license."

"You need a license to sell real estate?"

Whitney's voice was full of scorn at the ignorant reporter. "Yes, of course you do."

"Maybe somebody who had a license was in on it with him?" I suggested.

The disbelief again. "No, no, no."

"Why not?"

"Because, smart guy, the building was sold before James ever came to Magen & Burke."

"What?"

"That's right. It was sold in March. Bjorn didn't start working till, I don't know, April . . . May."

"Listen, Arch," I told him, "I know for a fact that James made that commission."

"How do you know?"

"An unimpeachable source."

"What?" Bewilderment was beginning to impinge on sarcasm. "I don't know what the hell kind of a story you're trying to cook up, but it's nonsense."

"Maybe so, but it's the truth."

"I'm going to look into this," Whitney declared. "Why don't you hold up on that story till I check on it?"

"Deal."

Actually, I couldn't have hoped for anything better.

"I'm going to put that punk in his place once and for all," he muttered.

I was going to say that somebody already had, but let it go.

19

AFTER WORK I walked down Third Avenue with Bike O'Malley to Kelly's, and filled Timmy in on Skates Stern's indictment.

"Glad to hear it," pronounced Timmy. "I hope he fries."

There's no death penalty in New York any more, but people still hope that killers fry.

I felt pretty glum about the whole damned thing. Skates obviously was a defendant who satisfied everybody — Detective Messina, Timmy, Kerry Burke. The only person who wasn't satisfied was me—and Skates— and our opinions didn't seem to count.

I managed to put the whole mess out of my mind by getting into a heated discussion about the incomprehensible fortunes of the New York Mets. And because of that, I didn't see how it started.

I didn't see the Green Dress come in, or see her sit beside Bike O'Malley at the bar. I only heard the uproar when it happened.

Bike O'Malley, you understand, admires Green Dresses, or any other color if they cling fetchingly to a female figure, as this one did to a voluptuous redhead with nice, long legs.

We heard something like, "Aarraahh!" or possibly, "You dirty son of a bitch!" And then a loud crunk-thump, as Bike and a large man went down on the floor.

Timmy went thump-thumping up to the front, and his

bartender, Little Denny, went over the bar, and I came up behind them, and there were Bike O'Malley and the large stranger rolling around cursing and trying to put each other out of commission.

Little Denny, who's six-three, shoved them apart long enough for the stranger to get up and pull out a gun and a gold detective shield.

"Police officer," he yelled rudely, apparently annoyed at everybody in Kelly's, and Bike O'Malley in particular.

Bike got up, slowly, glaring at the cop and considering whether he wanted to pay attention to the gun. Denny got in front of him, and so did I. Because Bike is even bigger than Little Denny.

Through all this, the Green Dress was screeching like one possessed, dancing around and calling the cop unladylike things such as "pig," "rotten creep," and "scummy fuzz."

"What the hell's going on?" Timmy finally was able to ask during a lull.

"What's going on is a hooker and a john," declared the red-faced cop, glaring at O'Malley and Green Dress.

"Who's a john?" O'Malley wanted to know. He looked confusedly at the Green Dress. "Hooker?"

"So what?" she came back defiantly.

Well, the cop was Detective McGuire of the Public Morals Squad, and he was taking in the hooker for soliciting and Bike O'Malley for treating him with physical disrespect, otherwise known as felonious assault.

"How'd I know you were a cop?" Bike protested. "You grabbed the broad, so—"

"Another hooker?" Timmy was aghast. He stepped over to her. "What are you doing in here? What is this?"

"Screw off," said the hooker evenly.

When Detective McGuire discovered Bike was a reporter and so was I, he calmed down a little. Arresting a reporter is always trouble for a cop, so he finally agreed to take in only the hooker.

That should have made us all feel a lot better, but Timmy was in a frightful tizzy. "Jesus," he kept saying.

"Hell, I'm sorry," Bike told him, looking hangdog. "I didn't know she was a hooker. You never had them in here."

Bike O'Malley explained what had happened to him, and it was pretty much a carbon copy of what had happened to me with the first hooker.

"She put one hand on my leg and the other on my money," said Bike. "And because of the one hand, I didn't think about the other one."

"Where are they coming from?" I asked, stupefied by the trouble this could cause.

"Why, dammit, from the falling down buildings on the block," said Timmy furiously. "I had to throw an underage kid out of here the other day."

I was trying to think. The other time when that hooker put her hooks into me, there had been a Public Morals Squad cop sitting beside her, too.

"Timmy, you think this is an accident? Cops and hookers in here at the same time on both occasions?"

"Not any more, I don't, goddammit," snapped Timmy. "Two hooker arrests! They can lift my license!"

"Aw, they wouldn't do that," Bike said, looking like a thoroughly whipped mongrel. "Hell, you been here forever."

"They wouldn't?" Timmy raged. "Not much, they wouldn't. They been after me for months, now."

"Who's been after you?" I asked.

"Everygoddambody! Inspectors in and out! The damned landlord trying to break my lease. Now they're sending in hookers!"

"Wait a minute, Timmy. Who's sending in hookers?"

"How the hell do I know? But I'll bet it's that's bastard of a landlord."

Timmy explained that while he had ten years still to go on a fifteen-year lease, a new owner had bought the property about a year ago and had been after him to give up the lease.

"Damn, why didn't my father buy the property when he could?" Timmy mourned. "He could've gotten it for peanuts thirty-forty years ago."

"You think the landlord's trying to get your license?"

"I know it. He tried to buy me out three times. I don't know what the hell he wants to put in here—a massage parlor, for all I know. Well, I'm not getting out! I promised my father I'd keep the place and pass it on to—" He trailed off then. "Godammit, if you ain't got your own place, you're just a croppy."

"Who is this landlord?" I asked him.

"I don't know. Some damned company . . . Limited Development Company or something. They sent a twerp of a fast-talking lawyer around to buy up the lease. I told the runt to take a flying leap for himself. What would I do without the store?"

"Retire to Florida?"

"Huh! Retire! You retire and then you die."

"Listen, Timmy, I'll tell 'em what happened," said a hangdog Bike O'Malley. "Fitz and I'll tell them."

"Yeah, you're gonna have to," said Timmy.

I left Kelly's and walked to my Mustang parked up by the *Daily Press*, thoroughly befuddled. No sooner had we managed to clear up James's murder—if it *was* cleared up —when somebody tries to get Timmy tossed out.

I was still plunged in confused thought when I got to the Mustang. I climbed in and was leaning over, sticking the key into the ignition.

CRASH!

An explosion of glass at my left window. Something sprinkling the left side of my face like a thousand stinging bees.

I didn't know what had happened. I remembered once I stepped off a subway platform and my right foot went all the way to rail bed, my left knee buckling under me, and my head hit the concrete platform. Disorientation. You can't get your bearings.

I shot a terrified look at the car window, and it was shattered into milky pulp. I was covered with grainy bits of glass.

Instinctively, I ducked away and opened the car door on the right side. Slide down into the gutter and crawl forward toward a car parked in front of me, head dizzy, confusion complete.

There were running steps and a muffled shout—"Goddamit!" or something. I glanced back and saw a shadow around the Mustang. Somebody was leaning in through the shattered window, looking for me.

"Shit!" I heard him spit again.

There's a parking garage on the same side of the street at that point, and I saw a car pulling up to go in. The big garage door slowly rose to let the car in.

Crawl frantically to the front of the parked car, and then sprint toward the garage door as it started back down. I went under it like Phil Simms, the Giants quarterback, sliding across the Astroturf at Giants Stadium to avoid being creamed by a mastodon of a lineman.

In under the big garage door on my face and chest, scraping skin and clothes, rolling the last couple of feet to avoid the goddamned door.

BAM!

Something thudded into the lower part of the door where I had just skittered through.

Running footsteps outside up to the garage door. Banging and thumping on it, deep breathing, a guttural curse.

"Please don't open the damned door," darting through my head as I lay there in shock.

Later, after whoever it was had gone, the cops and I found the splintered hole in the lower part of the garage door. The cops dug out a slug battered into a shapeless mass that had crashed into the wood. They found another one inside the Mustang.

20

THERE'S SOMETHING ABOUT being shot at that gets people's attention. You're put into a squad car and driven to the Nineteenth Precinct station house and dragged up to the squad room and put into a chair across from Detective Messina of the bent nose. But what he wants to know is not who shot at you, but what the goddam hell you're doing to get yourself shot at.

"What are you doing out there, Fitzgerald, playing James Garner?"

"Well . . . "

"What the hell are you doing bothering my witnesses?" he raced on. "And how did you find Kerry Burke?"

" . . . see . . . "

"Are you acquainted with a statute defined as witness tampering?" he snapped, pacing around behind his desk.

"Hey, Messina, wait a minute!" I was dabbing the right side of my face and forehead, which looked like hamburger before it's cooked.

"What'd you do to your face?" he asked in an annoyed voice.

"*I* didn't do *anything* to it," I said. "The goddam concrete under the garage door did it. When I was running for my life from some maniac who doesn't seem to interest you at all."

Well, I was wrong about that, all right. He was interested. Plenty interested.

"Why is somebody trying to shoot you?" is the way he put it.

"How am I supposed to know?" I complained. "You're the cop here."

Yes, declared Messina pompously, he was the cop, and it was way past time for me, a bumbling sap of an amateur, to realize it. How could he prepare his case when he kept hearing that I was out there ranging through the streets of the Big Apple, badgering citizens and browbeating witnesses?

"You mean Kerry?" I managed to say rather quietly. "How'd you find out about that?"

"How'd I find out?" Messina screeched, leaping to his desk like some kind of a clumsy grizzly bear. He snatched up a copy of the *Daily Press* and started waving it around.

"It's in the goddamned paper!" he finally howled.

"I didn't use her name," I protested. "Who's going to know?"

Messina gave me a long, smoldering glare. "Who's going to know? I'll tell you who. *Kerry!* And I'm telling you right now to stay away from her."

"What?"

"I've talked to her and managed to calm her down, but I had a helluva sweet time doing it." He leaned across the desk portentiously. "Do you know what happens to people who tamper with prosecution witnesses?"

"Tamper?"

"They get charged with obstruction of justice!"

That got my attention. Detective Messina was getting down to the bottom line. I was thinking of telling him that I had also talked to Kerry again, and that everything was all right now, but thought better of it.

"I was only trying to help," I muttered.

"Don't help!"

"But, see, Skates's story doesn't check out with Kerry's," I said.

"Of course not, goddamit!" Messina smoldered. "She's the main witness against him. He's lying through his teeth, for chrissake, but you listen to his fast-talking swill and put it in the paper. Or do you think Miss Burke is lying?"

Messina frowned, his dark face a mixture of disgust and forbearance.

"Kerry?" I asked dumbly.

"Yeah! If their stories don't match, one of them's lying. Is that what you're telling me? She made this story up? Why?"

"I didn't say that."

"Okay! Then get your head on straight and stop listening to a punk bookie who lies for a living!"

I sat there silently as his logic hammered me into a black spot.

"I'm trying to gather facts, quietly, and you keep broadcasting every goddam mixed-up, wrong scrap of bullshit you hear."

He looked downright frustrated. "Fitzgerald," he now asked in a strained and even pleading manner, "why do you keep putting these things in the paper?"

It was a silly question to ask me. "I'm a reporter," I explained.

Well, that was just too bad. I might be a gossiping, sensation-seeking, yellow-stained scribbler, but he was a peace officer and a detective of New York's Finest, and he would not have me splashing evidence all over the public prints to help slimy degenerates like Thomas J. "Skates" Stern from Allen Street, and that was that.

I got the distinct impression that we were at cross-purposes.

He paused, coming gradually down from the ceiling. He accomplished this by lighting a big, black cigar and puffing on it for a few moments. Then he looked at me again.

"Now, what the hell have you been up to?"

He sat in his chair across from me, glaring intently, waiting for my explanation. I felt like a French aristocrat facing Citizen Robespierre.

"Why is somebody trying to shoot you?" he said, finally coming around to what seemed to me the main point.

"I've been trying to figure that one out."

Messina smirked. "A jealous husband, maybe?"

"Cute."

"Well, then what?"

"I guess I must have been asking the wrong persons the right questions," I came back.

"Okay. Who have you been talking to?"

I tried to go over them in my mind. Skates Stern? He was in the Tombs, and that didn't make sense, anyway. Kerry Burke? Naw. She was helping me.

Archer Whitney? Why? Was it possible that Whitney had become so jealous of James's attentions to Kerry that he had killed him? I thought it over. Archer was big enough to have been that Cro-Magnon who took a shot at me.

"Naw," I muttered.

"Naw what?"

"Nothing." That goon hadn't been Archer. I had seen enough of him to know that.

Squeaky Duffy?

I must have made a sign when that thought hit me because Detective Messina was on his feet, around the desk, sitting on the edge to stare down at me with interest.

"Who'd you think of?"

"I'm not sure," I stalled. Squeaky Duffy? Had I spooked him down at Walsh's? He certainly would have

116

access to a gun. The shadowy form leaning into the pulpy window of my Mustang floated back into my head. I hadn't gotten a good look at the guy, that's for sure, but I saw enough to know it wasn't Duffy. The gunman was a big, tough-looking character, and his voice wasn't anything like Duffy's. But it could have been one of Duffy's minions who helped merchandise fall off trucks.

"Okay, look, the guy who Skates said sold him the gun is called Squeaky Duffy. He's got a desk in Walsh's next to Skates's."

Messina made a gesture and turned away. "We know about him," he said.

"What does he say?"

"I don't know. We can't find him," the detective muttered. "Probably because some buttinski talked to him, and now he's hiding out under the Coney Island boardwalk."

His sneer left no doubt who he thought that buttinski was.

"You think Duffy pegged that shot at you?" he asked.

I shrugged. "No."

"Why not? You were trying to tie him to the murder weapon. Why not?"

"Because I saw the guy, and he was a lot bigger, about the size of Mark Gastineau. It could have been one of his boys, though."

"Great." Messina meant the opposite. He stalked back behind his desk and threw some papers around. "Okay, we'll find Duffy sooner or later. I'll run the slugs through ballistics, but they're probably pretty mashed up. If you think of anything else, let me know."

"I can go?"

"Yeah, yeah," he said tiredly. "But for God's sake stay out of my case. Stick to writing weather stories."

I left and had to take a cab back across town to the East Side and my bombed-out Mustang. I certainly have a lot of luck with cars. I drove home with the wind whistling in, wishing the strong breeze would air out my brain so I could figure out what was going on. There was something bothering me, but I couldn't get it straight.

I put in a call to the city desk and filled in Rick, the night city editor, on my grilling at the hands of Messina. I had already told Ironhead about the bazooka that demolished the car window, and had asked him not to put anything in the paper about it just yet.

It wasn't until I hung up the phone that it suddenly hit me that somebody had tried to remove me from the world. My knees went weak and I slumped onto the sofa. It's funny the way danger only seems to penetrate your consciousness later, when you're perhaps better able to assimilate it.

I don't usually drink anything but beer, but on this occasion a good stiff slug of scotch was in order. I lit a Tiparillo, tossed off the scotch, and tried to think.

Obviously, somebody had dropped me a hint that my activities were annoying them, and that they wanted me to stop. But who? And why? I sat there in a blue funk and nothing occurred to me. My meanderings were finally interrupted by the phone.

"Fitz?" It was Buzz, the copy boy, who was manning the nightside switchboard at the paper.

"Yeah, Buzz."

"Listen, a guy called. I wouldn't give him your home number, so he asked you to call him back. Somebody Stern."

"Skates?"

"Yeah . . . sounded a little goofy."

Skates, all right. Buzz gave me the number and I dialed it right back.

"Yeah?" came a hushed reply.

"Skates?"

"Fitzgerald?" He was still speaking in a half-whisper. "Jesus, am I glad to hear from you. I'm in trouble."

"What'd you do—take bets inside the Tombs? And how come they let you take calls this late?"

"Huh?" he said, apparently confused. "Naw, I'm out on bail."

"Where are you?"

Skates didn't speak for a moment. Then he started talking so low I jammed the phone into my ear, straining to hear. "What?" I said.

"Fitz, I'm at Duffy's."

"What? Where?"

"In Brooklyn. I hadda come over here and get him to own up about that gun."

"Yeah? Well, what does he say?"

"Nothing!"

"What do you mean nothing?"

"I mean he's dead!"

I put my forehead in my left hand and tried to blot out what he had said.

"What do you mean, he's dead?" I finally managed.

"I came in and found him slumped over the kitchen table. There's a hole in his ear."

I wish I could tell you I did something sensible like hang up and notify Detective Messina. But instead I got the address from Skates and told him I'd be right out.

Jupiter, the Roman god of the heavens, apparently is in league with Murphy, of Murphy's Law, which states that anything that can go wrong will go wrong. Murphy's Law required that if I were driving on a dark night in a Mustang with a missing left front window, that it would rain. Jupiter heard Murphy and sent down sheets of water to pour in through the window.

I drove down the FDR Drive, and then over the Brooklyn Bridge and down into Flatbush almost to Prospect Park. Squeaky Duffy lived in one of those brick apartment houses off Flatbush Avenue. I rode a herky-jerky elevator up into the cabbage-smelling building, and knocked softly on the apartment door.

The door opened a crack, and Skates's nervous eyes looked warily out at me. I pushed in, and he closed the door.

Before I said a word, Skates nodded his head toward the kitchen. We were in a stuffy, dark living room. Skates hadn't turned on the lights. Dim light from a gas-range clock filtered in from the kitchen.

I took a couple of steps toward the kitchen and saw Squeaky Duffy slumped over the table, his face on the Formica top, dribbling blood from one ear. Beautiful.

I turned away. Skates had sunk onto a couch in the darkness, apparently petrified and immobilized. I sat across from him in a stuffed chair.

"What happened?" I finally was able to ask.

Skates threw up his hands, and for once was at a loss for words.

I wasn't bubbling with talk, either.

"Did you shoot him?" came from me at last.

Skates leaned forward and held his head. Then he straightened up and his hands were out to me, both palms up, a beseeching gesture. "Put me inna auto compactor! Shove me inna concrete mixer!"

"You mean you didn't shoot him."

"Trample me with horses!"

It certainly was lovely.

"Whatta we gonna do?" moaned Skates Stern, and I was getting sick and tired of his saying "we" when one of his bizarre peccadilloes desecrated the landscape.

But, of course, there was nothing *to* do except call the police and tell them.

"You ain't gonna let them pin this on me?" whined Skates.

Oh, no. Certainly not. He gets out on bail and goes

straight to the house of the man who sold him a gun that killed somebody. He finds the body, all by himself. Pin it on him? Why, Messina wouldn't even have to bother. The killing was stitched up and down Skates's back with a Singer sewing machine.

And there I was, right in it with the revolting little creep who had attached himself to me like a sucker fish on a shark. I wished I could find some horses so they *could* trample the goddamned wimp.

21

YOU KNOW HOW many people show up at a murder scene? Not less than five hundred. There are uniform cops from the Empire Boulevard station, detectives from the Empire Boulevard squad, assistant medical examiners, and even the police reporter from the *Daily Press* Brooklyn shack.

"Jeez, Fitz, what's going on?" Joey Dudley, the reporter, wanted to know, sliding up to me in the cramped living room.

"Oh, God," I muttered.

Joey's a tall drink of water who looks like a longshoreman dressed up like a process server. He wears a long, greenish sort of army-navy store trench coat and a hat down over his eyes.

"Rick calls and tells me to get over here," Dudley whispered to me out of the side of his mouth. "You mixed up in something again?"

I had put in a call to the city desk to alert Rick Massilli, the night city editor, about my situation.

"You're covering a murder in Brooklyn?" he had asked, somewhat bewildered.

"Not exactly, Rick. I'm just here."

"For God's sake, you didn't scrag the guy?" Rick had gone on.

"Aw, what are you talking about?"

"I don't know," Rick had snapped. "Suppose you tell me."

"It's a long story."

Rick had sighed. "Okay," he had said, plainly indicating that whatever it was, it was on my head.

So, Skates Stern and I had waited. I had turned on some lights and lit a Tiparillo, and tried to get some kind of a story out of the hyperventilating bookie.

"Listen," he had begun, "let's get out of here."

"Nobody's going anywhere."

"You tell 'em, then. I gotta go."

Skates had edged toward the apartment door, but I got in front of him and shoved him back across the room into a chair.

"You think you're taking off and leaving me holding the bag?" I demanded rather crossly.

"Throw me off the Brooklyn Bridge," he protested. "I don't know nothing!"

Skates's continuing lack of knowledge in the face of dead bodies was certainly a wonder. He calls on James Kelly, and then Kelly's dead and Skates's mind is a total blank. He goes to visit Squeaky Duffy, and Duffy is dead with a bullet in his ear, and Skates's mind is a vast, windswept desert. Unhappily, this time I was also there, and questions would be asked that would not be satisfied by offering to be thrown off a bridge.

"Goddamit, Skates, are you playing me for a sap?" I exploded.

"Put me before a firing squad!"

"They might, this time, you damned hoople! Now, tell me what happened."

Skates sat forward on the stuffed chair, folded his arms on his knees, and launched into an account that required a Japanese interpreter.

There he had been in the Tombs, "mobilized like some Irish skel from Red Hook," reaching out on the prison phone to anybody who would help. "Jimmy the Freeze owes me . . . Red the waitress is inta me . . . Solly

Metzger is on my pad for five hundred!" Would these black-hearted customers come up with any scratch so he could make bail? "Dump me down the sewer!"

"What about the stash under your ice cubes?"

"That's for emergencies."

"For *what?*"

"I got expenses! Household finance! People . . . what ya want from me. I can't touch it!"

"Goddamit, Skates . . . "

"Okay, so I call my mother. Do I carry her? Do I give her a hot tip on the Daily Double at Belmont? Does she want to get her son out of the goddamned dungeon?"

"I don't know, Skates," I said wearily. "Does she?"

"Only after she hollers like a pier boss!"

"The cops will be here, for chrissake," I yelled. "So you made bail and came here. Right?"

"I go by Walsh's, and is Duffy there? No! Somebody came and grilled him and he ain't been seen since."

I flinched a little at that. I must have been that somebody.

"So I get on the subway and beat it out here."

"What did you want with Duffy?"

What did he want? *What did he want?* "I gotta know is he gonna stand up and get me off the hook," Skates told me. "He's gotta tell the cops he got me that piece for somebody else. I gotta get my head outa the noose."

He had ridden the No. 4 IRT Lexington Avenue subway and scurried to Duffy's place. Nobody answered the bell, so he had gone up to Duffy's apartment. Still, nobody answered. So, Skates had tried the door. It was broken open.

"I come in, and right away I spot Duffy at the kitchen table, his face down on the top. I go up to him, and there he is being dead."

"That's all?"

"Sell me to the Arabs!"

Do you know how many vehicles show up at a murder scene? Not less than a hundred. Police sector cars, squad cars, an ambulance, an assistant ME's car. Even the car of a nosy reporter from my own paper.

They all came shoving in, each one wearing a face that said, "Well, well, what have we here?"

"What are *you* doing here?" was another question on their faces when they looked at me.

What I was doing there, of course, was getting my ass in a sling.

A detective from the Empire Boulevard squad determined that one Sylvester Duffy, aka Squeaky, was DOA at the kitchen table. This was confirmed by a rail-thin kid with a mustache in a white jacket who was an assistant Medical Examiner.

The detective, Morris McDonald, then determined that a subject identified as Edward Fitzgerald, aka Idiot, a member of the Fourth Estate from the *New York Daily Press,* had assisted one Thomas Sternweiss, turf accountant, in discovering the body.

Possibly my mind was trying to block out all the frightful disasters looming up before me, because I turned to Skates and asked, "Sternweiss?"

"That's my real name," he admitted.

But that was, as a lawyer would say, irrelevant and immaterial in the presence of a newly deceased body. More to the point, said Detective McDonald, was what I was doing there.

I told him.

He turned to Skates Sternweiss, lately of the Tombs. What was *he* doing there?

Skates told him.

"How's that again?" McDonald wanted to know.

Joey Dudley, the reporter, sidled up to me again and hissed in my ear. "What'd that little bookie say?"

"Don't ask."

"But I got to phone in some kind of a story to Rick . . . unless you want to file?"

"No, no, leave me out of it."

Joey Dudley gave me a pained look. "How?"

"I got here afterward," I suggested.

"Oh." Joey shuffled his feet uncomfortably. "Well, okay, I'll unload to Rick and he can handle it. He says Ironhead has to be left a memo, too."

Dudley shuffled out of the apartment, looking none too happy. Well, I wasn't happy either. All I needed was Ironhead's participation. I thought of letting Skates talk to him, and that made me smile just a bit.

Well, we were all transported over to the Empire Boulevard station house and taken up into the squad room, where Detective McDonald stood over to one side, whispering with another man. I heard little bits of the conversation.

" . . . reporter . . . bookie . . . shot in the ear . . . smashed window in his car . . . "

He was rather chubby with a sort of Charlie Chaplin mustache and a blue suit, and he was affable and suspicious at the same time.

"Mark Bernstein. I'm the assistant district attorney."

He sort of grinned at me, partly amused, partly ominous, and his manner declared that while I might be a newspaper reporter in my civilian life, I was at the moment nothing more or less than a person under investigation.

"Would you like to give me a statement?" he asked politely.

"I've got nothing to hide," I ventured recklessly.

"Good." Polite smile with a touch of amused malevolence behind the gray, steady eyes.

"Maybe I oughta tell Rick, so he can get Corcoran," offered Joey Dudley, who was sitting beside me on a bench in the squad room.

126

"Corcoran?" asked blue suit.

"Company lawyer," I said. All I needed was sad-faced, nervous Charles W. Corcoran, the *Daily Press* lawyer, coming down on me. Corcoran had a way of looking over your left shoulder when he talked to you, and what he usually said was, "Oh, my goodness!"

Dudley went off to call Rick, which would set in motion a ghastly cavalcade of *Daily Press* officials, from itchy Corcoran to unstable Ironhead to shadowy Mr. McFadden, the publisher, to who-the-hell-knows who else.

While my fate went singing over the telephone wires from the police station to the *Daily Press,* and then onward to the slumbering Corcoran and the snoring Ironhead, a message from the trenches sure to cause consternation and havoc for me eventually, Mark Bernstein turned his attention to Skates.

"Would you like to give me a statement?" Bernstein asked him.

"I don't know nothin'! All I did was collect my money, and I didn't hear no shots," Skates launched in. "Duffy was already shot when I got there which I can't shed no light on."

Bernstein frowned and went over to whisper to Detective McDonald, who let out a little laugh.

"You got me into this, you gotta get me out," Skates burbled at me.

"Shut up!" I'm afraid I croaked.

"Why'n't I stay in the deli?" Skates mourned.

"What deli?"

"I useta deliver for my Uncle Sid's deli on roller skates."

Well, that cleared up his nickname.

"He ast me why do I wanta be a bookie when I can stay in his deli! Do I listen?"

"I don't know. Did you?"

"Can bagels fly?"

Bernstein and McDonald came back, read Skates his rights, and told him that he could make a statement, if he chose, or he could contact legal counsel.

"All of a sudden, everybody wants me to get a lawyer!" Skates wailed. "I didn't do nothin'."

"You want to give us a statement?"

"Sure! Only I don't write so good. Can I tell ya?"

Detective McDonald pulled Bernstein away to talk, and then they came back.

"I think you'd better write it yourself."

A deep, pitiful groan emanated from Skates Stern, but he took the yellow pad Bernstein offered him and bent over to put down the tenuous tale of how he had been so foully used by fate and circumstance.

During it, we all sat there in the squad room, drinking coffee and smoking and waiting to hear from Corcoran. He finally called and talked with Bernstein, and they worked something out. I could go, but I would be expected to make myself available later to give a statement in the presence of counsel.

"How'd he sound?" I asked Bernstein.

"Not happy," the chubby ADA smiled.

As for Skates, he labored over his yellow pad, trying to put down something coherent, but eventually gave up and talked instead into a tape recorder, interrupted endlessly by a more and more frustrated Mark Bernstein.

"I've never heard anybody talk like that," he said once to a grinning McDonald.

"He doesn't talk," said McDonald. "He runs off at the mouth."

When Skates finally finished his statement, such as it was, he was told he was being detained.

"For what?" he complained.

Detective McDonald conferred whisperingly with Bernstein.

"Burglary."

"What burglary? I didn't take nothing!"

Bernstein explained that he didn't have to take anything. Breaking and entering Duffy's apartment made it burglary.

"I didn't break, I just entered!"

"The door was broken in, Skates," said McDonald.

"Not by me."

Even if they couldn't get him for burglary, which they certainly could, explained Bernstein, they had him for trespassing and suspicion of murder.

"I didn't touch Duffy!" Skates howled.

That would be determined in due course, said Bernstein. But in the meantime, Skates would be a guest at the Brooklyn House of Detention.

"But I just got outa the Tombs on bail."

McDonald and Bernstein looked at each other. "Why were you in the Tombs?" asked Bernstein.

"I decline to answer on the grounds that I don't understand what is going on and my mother will yank out my fingernails."

McDonald looked inquiringly at me.

"For God's sake, Skates," I said, "you can't hide a murder indictment."

"Ahhhhhhh!" screeched Skates. "Lousy canary!"

Bernstein's eyes widened. " Murder?"

"I didn't do it," Skates said, sinking into a chair. "Ask Fitzgerald! He got me into this."

It took another half hour to go through the whole damned James Kelly thing, and Detective Messina's name was brought up, and I was beginning to wish I had stayed on the loading dock with my teamster father.

Naturally, Detective McDonald had to call the Nineteenth Precinct to reach bent-nose Messina, who had gone home. So he called Messina at home and told him the whole Sargasso Sea tale, and was in turn told by

Messina that they had been looking for Duffy. How Skates had gotten past the cops that were supposedly staked out at Duffy's apartment remained to be determined, but was probably simple enough: the cops had taken a coffee break, or had gotten tired of waiting. Anyway, the conclusion to the calls was that Detective McDonald told Skates:

"So you got to Duffy before we did, huh?"

"Drown me in Sheepshead Bay!"

So Skates was put into a holding cell, now likely facing another charge of murder, and I was told I could leave.

"Messina wants you at the precinct tomorrow," was McDonald's ominous send-off at about three in the morning.

I went outside to the Mustang and drove back out of Brooklyn, stopping at a newsstand near Prospect Park for a *Daily Press*. Joey Dudley had phoned in a short story about Sylvester Duffy being murdered, and saying a suspect was in custody. Skates wasn't mentioned by name, and neither was I.

I drove back to Manhattan, and Jupiter and Murphy were still at it, whipping rain into my face all the way back to East Eighty-second Street.

22

YOU KNOW HOW it is when you're so bone tired you ache for sleep but are so tensed up that you keep twitching and jerking yourself awake to stare at the clock and realize that only a couple of minutes have gone by? That's the way I was that morning after coming home from Brooklyn.

What I wanted was to forget the whole thing, but what I would face when morning came would be a regular concatenation of abuse, accusation, and outrage. Wearily, I closed my eyes and tried to slip into the River Lethe, the stream of unconsciousness the ancient Romans called sleep. But the river led to an ocean, and the ocean bottom was littered with sunken wrecks.

There was a school of codfish darting in and out through the rusty remains of my relationship with Detective Messina. By morning I would be called upon to explain to him how in the double-dyed hell I had stumbled upon a new murder of yet another witness in this hopelessly bollixed up case. That particular wreck spread through the lower bottom of my tortured mind like the immense, twisted carcass of the *Titanic*. I averted my gaze.

And there was another blasted undersea shape, inhabited by the white, tangled form of a giant squid, ready to envelop me in darkest ink if I approached too closely. That was Ironhead, stirring up wrath with a memo from Rick Massilli. I twitched away.

There was a capsized tugboat, air bubbles escaping from some roiling compartment inside, and that was Charles W. Corcoran, skipper of the *Daily Press* legal department. I winced.

There, half-buried in sand, a pirate galleon hiding a snapping moray eel, was the hopeless mess that was Skates Stern and his idiotic array of troubles. Don't get too close to that tar baby of the deep, or there would be no escape, ever.

And finally, a great, gray shark glided ominously around a scuttled battleship, eying me through the murky depths—the lout who had tried to transport me to Davy Jones's locker with a gun.

And slipping through it all was a new ichthyological wonder—a bell fish. It puffed itself up and gave off a strident clanging. I came awake with a start, shaken out of a barely recognizable nightmare.

I stared at the phone and realized there was virtually nobody on the other end that I wanted to talk to. Certainly none of those hulking inhabitants of the deep who only wanted to eviscerate me for a dozen possible felonies.

When I finally answered it, this is what I got:

"Get your ass in here!"

Ironhead Matthews in a state of combustibility.

I shaved and dressed and splashed my face with Old Spice, trying to shock myself awake. Then I drove over to Second Avenue and into John the Chevron man's place. I was sick and tired of the wind and the rain pouring in on me through the totaled driver's-side window. I asked John to put in a new window and, while he was at it, to remove all that shiny chrome from underneath that produced a vroom every time I started up, and the humped-up springs that kept me looking downhill all the time.

"Somebody put a lot of dough into this thing," John marveled. "You want all that taken off?"

"Yeah, John. Off."

He scratched his head. "Cost a lot to take it all off, too."

Naturally.

I took the subway down to the *Daily Press* and walked cautiously into the city room, where Ironhead sat at his desk waiting for me like a cherry bomb with the fuse sticking out of it.

The great Grucci family could have taken Ironhead out to Shea Stadium, lit the fuse, and they would have produced the greatest fireworks display they ever had.

"Get the hell over here!" was the way he started.

He had a memo from Rick Massilli in front of him on his desk, and he was looking at me with his neck crooked, and that vein in his forehead was already throbbing.

"What the hell is this?" He flapped a sheet of paper.

"You mean about Squeaky Duffy?" I asked innocently.

"No . . . yes . . . no . . . goddamit!"

"Didn't Joey Dudley write that story?"

"Joey . . . ? What the hell were you *doing* out there?"

"Well, Skates called me, and—"

"They want a statement!"

"Who?"

"*Who?* The goddam Brooklyn District Attorney's office! Corcoran's having kittens. And what the hell did you do to that detective?"

"You mean Messina?"

Ironhead leaped to his feet, unable to sit there calmly, and stomped around by his desk. Suddenly I realized the entire city room was silent. You couldn't even hear the discreet blip-blip of the VDT machines. Fitzgerald the screw-up was being turned rapidly on a spit, and everyone was simply delighted.

"You're supposed to be a reporter, Fitzgerald," Ironhead was raving, "a reasonably sane, organized gatherer and writer of facts! But what are you?"

I wasn't sure this was an actual question.

"You're a nut case!"

I was right.

"You go careening around to the Tombs and out to Brooklyn and have goddam detectives and ADAs calling me up in the middle of the night and half the time there isn't even a decent story in it."

"Well, see, I didn't think much of it, either, until that guy tried to shoot me."

Ironhead fairly catapulted to his desk and grabbed up another piece of paper, which he shoved into the air for emphasis.

"Yes, and who's trying to kill you? That's another thing."

"There must be more to this story than I thought."

"*What . . . ?*"

"I said—"

"Shut up!"

My sentiment precisely.

Well, Ironhead admitted explosively that he didn't know what in the frazzle-assed world he was supposed to do about me. He had a newspaper to run and did not have the time or patience to deal with nut cases, and I had better go talk to Charles W. Corcoran, the newspaper lawyer, and then to the ADA in Brooklyn and then to Detective Messina and then take a flying fuck at the moon. In any order I wished.

Slowly, like the space shuttle *Columbia* returning to Earth, Ironhead glided downward, reentering the atmosphere in a flaming fireball, coasting gradually through the clouds and coming to rest finally at his desk. He looked at the memo and the other indictments before him, shoved them angrily aside, and stared at me.

"Fitz, what's going on?" he said almost wheedlingly.

I pulled up a chair and sat across from him, pausing to light a Tiparillo and organize my thoughts.

"I thought it was about the money."

"Money?"

"The $350,000 that was paid to James."

"James Kelly had 350 grand?"

"Right. So I thought . . . "

Ironhead grabbed up the *Daily Press*. "There's nothing about that in Dudley's story."

"No, it was earlier . . . "

"Earlier?"

"Messina said James earned it, and so does Kerry Burke."

"Kerry Burke?" Ironhead's forehead vein began throbbing again. He snatched up a paper, threw it aside, and snatched up another. "Kerry Burke is the mystery witness that this detective says he's going to lock you up for if you ever speak to her again and you're speaking to her again?"

"Messina said that?"

Ironhead held his head and said very softly, "Yes. What do you think I'm trying to tell you?" Softness climbed to harshness. "He was on my phone this morning screaming like a Muslim warrior." Harshness inclined toward raging.

"When did he call?"

Ironhead didn't know that. It was either before or after or between other calls from the ADA and Corcoran and a totally different detective from Empire Boulevard and from that demented bookie.

"Skates called, too?"

"Five times!"

"What'd he want?"

"He wants you to get him out of the Tombs so he can go out and kill somebody else!"

"Skates is back in the Tombs?"

Ironhead's eyes rolled. He looked at the ceiling. "Jesus H. Christ."

"I figured Skates—"

"Get out of here!"

"What?"

"Out!" Ironhead was on his feet doing an imitation of Ralph Kramden throwing Ed Norton out of his apartment. His arm rose and pointed. "Out!"

"What do you want me to do?"

"I don't know! I don't care! I want you to talk to all these people, and figure it all out, and then write me a story, and leave me the hell alone."

"Oh."

After that I went into Corcoran's office off the city room, and when he saw me he put his left hand over his left eye as though he had a headache.

"Oh, my goodness," he breathed, and told me to sit. I sat.

We worked up a statement for Detective McDonald of the Empire Boulevard station and for Mark Bernstein, the Brooklyn ADA. Corcoran said he hoped fervently that it would be accepted and that the integrity of the *Daily Press* would not be endangered.

He warned me to avoid talking to the New York City Police Department in general and Detective Messina in particular.

"But how can I cover the story if I can't talk to anybody?"

"Are you still on the story?" Corcoran was perplexed.

"Ironhead told me to get to the bottom of it."

"I would caution you to stay away from any witnesses or principals in this matter," he advised.

A lot of sense that made. Ironhead told me to get to

the bottom of it, but Corcoran tells me not to talk to anybody.

Even after leaving Corcoran it wasn't finished. I had to call Detective Messina. It sounded like a tape play-back, because this is what I got:

"Get your ass up here!"

I took the Lexington IRT Local subway up to the Nineteenth Precinct and told Messina everything that had happened with Skates and Squeaky Duffy in Brooklyn.

"Are you satisfied?" he demanded, which didn't give me much room for a response.

"Just confused," I finally said.

Well, Detective Anthony Messina of New York's Finest wasn't confused. It was all very simple, and he would explain it to me whether I wanted to hear it or not.

"Thomas J. "Skates" Sternweiss, a low-level bookie, met James Kelly at the Monkey Bar in the Elysee Hotel while making his rounds and realized he had met a fish. Soon, Skates was taking money off James on long-shot bets.

"Your friend James walked around like an extension of the Federal Reserve Bank," he explained.

All that cash set off an alarm in Skates Stern's greedy little brain, and he decided to rob him. But for that he needed a gun. Enter Sylvester "Squeaky" Duffy, loan shark and gun supplier.

Skates got a gun from Duffy, went to James's apartment, and robbed him. But since James knew Skates, he had to kill him.

But, that phone call from James to Kerry Burke ruined things. All of a sudden, Skates was in trouble. He tried to drag Duffy into it, claiming it was Duffy's gun and that Duffy must have killed James.

When it looked like Duffy was going to cave in and

testify against Skates, Skates did the natural thing. He removed Duffy.

"So now do you see why I didn't want Kerry Burke identified?" he bombasted at me.

"Yeah," I had to admit.

"She would have been next," he added unnecessarily.

I felt bad enough about that, already.

"Has Skates admitted everything?" I said.

"He will." Messina went back to his desk and sat down, apparently contented that the thing was all wrapped up.

"When he sees what we've got, he'll cop a plea," said the bent-nose detective. "And you stay away from him."

He didn't have to tell me that. I wanted nothing more to do with that boil on the rump of civilization. He still didn't seem like a killer to me, but then I wasn't a psychologist, and the evidence coming down on him was like an avalanche rumbling down the slope of the Jung-frau.

"What about the guy who took a shot at me?" I asked.

"Working on that," said Messina. "We're pretty sure it was one of Duffy's guys."

A cold chill went through me. "You mean Duffy was gunning for me?"

"Hell, yes! You went down there and tried to tie the gun to him. What did you expect?"

So that's what comes from trying to help out a friend.

I rode glumly back down to the *Daily Press* on the Lexington Avenue subway and wrote a story about Skates and Duffy. And I promised myself that the next time anything like this happened, I would call Dubbs Brewer at the police bureau and let him handle it.

I called Timmy Kelly and gave him a quick fill-in.

"Just as I thought . . . robbery," said Timmy.

"Yeah."

"Well, thanks, Fitz," he said. "And listen, I'm gonna need you to go to the S.L.A. with me."

"The State Liquor Authority?"

"Yeah. On those hookers that approached you and O'Malley."

"Sure, Timmy. What's new with that?"

"Hearing on Tuesday."

"Think you're in trouble?" I asked.

"I don't know, Fitz. It's the damndest thing. You'll be there?"

"Sure, Timmy."

After that I dawdled around and checked my phone messages. I was putting off making one last call. Glenn, the switchboard guy, had a message from Archer Whitney at Magen & Burke, but when I called he was out.

And then there was no help for it. I was back to the Romance of Buildings or make that last call.

"Fitz?" came Kerry Burke's voice bubbling over the phone.

"Yeah. Listen, can I talk to you?"

"Sure!" she breathed enthusiastically.

I got the feeling she had heard from Detective Messina.

"You heard about Skates?"

"God, it's such a relief," she said in a rush. "I can stop worrying. It's all over."

"Drink?"

"You're on! Where?"

Inspiration seized me. "Ever been to Windows on the World on top of the World Trade Center?"

"No! Sounds wonderful."

"It is."

I would explore the Romance of Buildings from the top of the world and do a little romancing of my own. Something good had come of it, after all.

23

I DON'T KNOW if you've ever been in the little bar on top of the World Trade Center. You look out at the East River from a hundred stories up and see a toy Brooklyn Bridge twinkling with greenish blue lights, with the River Cafe under it on the Brooklyn side.

And if you're sitting at a window table with dancing green eyes in a meltingly lovely Celtic face, the wonder of the Big Apple can overwhelm you.

We had a million things to talk about, of course. Mostly about Squeaky Duffy, Skates, and James. Kerry leaned across the table eagerly, hungry for details.

"I went crazy waiting for you to call," she breathed.

A happy little spasm went through me. "Really?"

"Yes! What happened?"

"Didn't Messina tell you?"

"Not really. Just not to worry about anything I see in the news, and that Skates Stern was in jail again. I didn't know he was out."

"Well, it was a mess," I said. "I guess I've been playing the damn fool all along, because now Skates has killed that guy out in Brooklyn."

Kerry seemed to freeze. Her pretty mouth hung open and she stared at me. "What?"

"Yeah. That guy who provided the gun—Squeaky Duffy."

Kerry couldn't seem to grasp it. "Duffy . . . Brooklyn . . . Skates Stern *killed* him?"

"Yeah. So much for my instinct."

Kerry was shaking as she sat there, finally aware of how much danger had been hovering over her.

"Oh, my God . . . "

I told her about my trip to Duffy's and to the Empire Boulevard station in Brooklyn.

"They've really got Skates this time?" she asked tremulously.

"Hog tied."

"So it was all a robbery, then?"

"Yeah. You must have misunderstood what James and Skates were talking about, or it was just a bet."

Kerry sat back and lit a cigarette, although she had one already burning in the ashtray. She was disoriented, I could see. She must have been experiencing that same feathers-in-the-brain sensation I went through when it finally hit me that somebody tried to kill me.

"You all right?" I asked.

" . . . what . . . ?"

"Look, you probably won't even have to testify now. I'm sorry I dragged you into this."

Finally she came around and heard me. A sweet, little smile played across her mouth, and I thought she was fighting back tears.

"You're a sweet guy," she murmured, and it went right through me.

"Maybe we can see each other some time, now that this is over," I ventured hopefully.

"Yes," she rushed out. "Yes . . . I don't want to be alone, Fitz. I've got to get away."

"Away?" My heart sank.

"My father bought a place on the Cape. It's mine now."

"Ought to be nice this time of year," I said wistfully.

"I can't go alone, Fitz. I feel so . . . I can't believe what's happened!" She was crying.

"Hey."

"Will you go with me?" she said then, looking up at me appealingly.

I wasn't sure I had heard her correctly. The glorious Kerry was inviting me to Cape Cod with her for the weekend?

"You want me to?" Still unable to believe it.

"Yes! Oh, yes, Fitz. I feel safe with you."

I didn't entirely like that characterization, but it didn't matter, not when I faced a fetching Celtic dream, lovely enough to force Ulysses to break free from the mast as he sailed past the Siren and heard her ululating cry.

"When?"

"Right now."

"Sure, I'll go," I finally managed.

"Thanks," she breathed.

Helpless. Marc Antony in Alexandria staring into the lavender eyes of Cleopatra.

We rode down in the elevator, her hand in mine, and I don't remember the descent at all. In a cab going uptown, she was in my arms, and her kiss dizzied me. She clutched me against her in a sort of frantic frenzy.

We had to take her car, a blue Triumph, because mine was at John the Chevron man's place on Second Avenue being stripped of chrome and humped-up springs. But Kerry didn't mind. We threw some things into suitcases and headed the Triumph up Interstate 95 and onto the New England Thruway.

It was glorious to be on the road with a smiling, black-haired Irish damosel beside me, her lovely face relaxed, her hand holding mine on the car seat. It was September, Indian summer in New England, and the nicest time of year in the northeast. Only a few hours earlier my chest had been constricted, my head in a vise, and now I felt like the Count of Monte Cristo emerging from the waves and declaring, "The world is mine."

I wish I could adequately describe that weekend on the Cape. We walked along the almost deserted beaches, holding hands and shyly glancing at each other. She was wearing gray slacks and an Irish fisherknit sweater that tried unsuccessfully to conceal her slender curves. Kerry clung to me, always touching me, holding my hand when we walked, snuggling up against me when we sat on the sand.

She talked and talked and talked. A jag of nonstop conversation about her life, about her late father, about Smith, about Arch. Not James, though. She wouldn't talk about him, or about work, either.

"Daddy wasn't tough enough," she told me. "He shouldn't have been in real estate. He should have been a teacher."

"What happened with him?"

She frowned and looked away. "I don't know. There was a deal that went sour, and I guess it was his fault. He killed himself, Fitz. God, let's not talk about that."

She pressed herself against me and kissed me with that same almost frantic urgency I had felt in the taxicab in New York. She couldn't get close enough to me.

We sat on the beach until very late, watching the constellations coming into view. You can't see them in New York, with all the obliterating lights around, but on the Cape you realize they're still there, swimming through their vast world—Orion the Hunter, the Big Dipper, Venus—oblivious to murders and city editors.

Back in the weather-beaten cottage, we sat in front of a fire and she tuned in an FM radio music station from Boston.

The suddenness of our coming together kept me in a rather bewildered state. I guess I stared at her bemusedly quite a lot because she sat up and looked into my eyes and smiled mischievously.

"What are you thinking?" Her eyes glowed.

"What do you think?"

She squinted her face at me. "I liked you from the first moment."

"Me, too."

She laughed softly and came close to me, and we kissed endlessly on the rug in front of the fire, and I probably spoke a good deal of romantic madness.

"Oh, Eddie," she murmured, "I think I love you," and the world came to a stop.

"Kerry . . ."

All right, I've never claimed I wasn't a fool about women. I knew she didn't love me. She was only a frightened woman reaching out for a safe harbor. I happened to be it. I wish I could tell you I had the strength to hold her off, to talk sense to her, but that's not the way it was. I slid into the Irish Sea and floated away.

We made love in a lumpy bed. She strained against me as though grafting us together, her arms holding me with surprising strength.

"I know you don't love me," she murmured once, and galaxies wheeled inside my own disordered mind.

"Kerry . . ."

"It's all right."

A strange girl, I thought. But there was time now.

If she felt safe in my arms, I felt positively weightless in hers. I was at peace finally about it all, my confusions swept away in the astonishing female wonder of her unimaginable, touching presence.

I was glad that Kerry was letting all the tension and misery slide out of her in my embrace. My troubles were going the same way. I felt a vast relief, even though I was sorry I had been wrong about Skates and had caused so much trouble as a result. But it was gone now, and I remembered Messina telling me why I had been wrong about Skates, about why he had to be lying. I hadn't even considered it until the moment he said it; that it was

Skates's word against Kerry's, and after that everything had become clear.

We loved and swam and looked our troubles out of each other, and no phones rang. It was an ending and a beginning.

24

BACK IN THE city on Monday morning, I awakened feeling marvelous, the warm, sunny glow of Kerry and the Cape still nestling inside me. Kerry and I were at last an item, and Skates and James Kelly were out of my head.

I walked over to Second Avenue to John the Chevron man's place, humming some mooncalf love song.

"Okay," John said. "All done."

I looked at my Mustang, and it was an ordinary, sleek, sweet-looking little 1978 job now, sitting low to the ground. It was still dusty, but I would get it washed one day—maybe. Off I went downtown in my refurbished chariot, feeling more or less brand new. The happy glow lasted until I got to the *Daily Press* and checked my desk calendar.

1. Buildings.
2. S.L.A. hearing tomorrow.

Instead of dealing with either one, though, I called Kerry at work and we laughed together for a while about our weekend, and we made plans to see each other the next night.

Buildings. God save me!

I checked my phone messages, and there were two more from Archer Whitney, apparently from the previous Friday evening. One of them said, "We were both right."

Right about what?

I called Whitney, but he wasn't in.

There sat the note about the S.L.A. hearing the next day. It glared at me and accused me. I had helped get Timmy Kelly into this mess, and I knew I had to try to get him out of it again. Until that loose end was tied up, I wasn't out of things with Timmy yet.

I remembered watching a nature documentary, the kind I call a bug show, on TV. It showed a bee lighting on a reed at the edge of a pond that hung down low over the water. The bee was alert for danger from all sides as he crawled on the reed. But then an archer fish under the surface squirted a stream of water up and knocked the bee into the pond, where the fish ate it. The bee wasn't expecting an attack from a lousy fish.

Well, that's the way this business of hookers in Kelly's struck me. What was going on? There we had been trying to find out what happened to James, and the next thing anybody knew Timmy was in danger of losing his place.

A little advance preparation was necessary for that hearing. Such as trying to find out what the hell had happened. I put in a call to Detective McGuire at the Public Morals Squad about those two hookers. He wasn't what you'd call overly cooperative.

"McGuire here."

"This is Fitzgerald, *Daily Press*. How you doing?"

Silence.

"Listen, I wanted to ask you about those hooker arrests."

Finally he spoke up. "I should have run that donkey in," he sulked.

"Aw, hell, he didn't know," I said, trying to soothe him. "Could you tell me how you happened to go to Kelly's looking for hookers?"

"It wasn't the first time," said the detective.

"I know. One of them got me the first time."

"You?" McGuire sounded a little happier. "You reporters all got hot pants, huh?"

I let that pass. "Who told you there were hookers at Kelly's?" I tried again.

"Let me see," he said, and shuffled papers. "Anonymous call. Said girls were working out of there. So, the boss sent us in."

Anonymous caller. Terrific. Timmy didn't know there were hookers in his place, but some anonymous caller did.

"Can you identify the two defendants for me?"

McGuire shuffled his papers again, and he had it.

The Green Dress who had bedazzled Bike O'Malley was Cecelia Waldrop, and her address was on Second Avenue around the block from Kelly's. The other one, who had laughed so toothsomely at my jokes, was Wanda Wrightson, and her address was on the side street a few doors away from Kelly's.

"What happened to them?" I asked.

"Disposition on the first one was . . . uh . . . fine."

"She's out again?"

"Yeah. Wrightson probably got a fine, too."

Wonderful. The hookers pay a hundred or two and walk out, but Timmy Kelly stands to lose his liquor license and his business.

I wish I could tell you that it all came together in my thick head at that point, but the fact is I still didn't know what was going on.

After talking to McGuire from the *Daily Press* city room that morning, I drove down to Kelly's and walked across the side street toward Second Avenue to try to find Wanda Wrightson. What I wanted to ask her was why she happened to go into Kelly's, and why she had seemed so eager to get herself busted. Because it had occurred to me that it was a most convenient coincidence that both times hookers tried to pick up johns, there were Public Morals Squad detectives sitting right beside them.

Maybe Wanda could tell me who the "anonymous" caller was who sent those dicks into Kelly's just at the right time. In other words, two accidental hooker arrests one on top of the other didn't add up to an accident to me.

It was the first time I had actually paid much attention to the block, other than to notice that there were several old brick apartment buildings boarded up, and some others undergoing demolition. I walked along until I got to the address Wanda had given. It was a swaying old tenement, probably built near the turn of the century, with a scarred stoop in front leading up to a battered old wooden front door with no lock on it.

The warped old green door swung open at my touch and banged against the wall. Inside, the place was a disaster. Cracked and crumbling plaster walls, a rickety wooden stairway leading upward that didn't look safe. There were no listings for the tenants, but I saw a piece of cardboard taped to one door.

"Super."

I took that to be the superintendent's apartment and knocked on it. There was raucous music blaring from inside.

The door suddenly flung open, and a large, scowling man stood there glaring at me. Some super. He didn't look like he would inspire much confidence in the tenants.

"Yeah?" He gave me a challenging look.

"I'm looking for Wanda Wrightson."

"She don't live here," he barked, and started to close the door. I put my hand out to stop him.

"Wait a minute," I said, annoyed. "The police say she does live here."

The brawny hulk gave me a closer look then. An

unshaven, surly face with alert eyes, and a distinctly bullying attitude.

"She moved," he snapped, and this time he shut the door before I could stop him or ask anything more.

I walked up that slanty staircase to the second floor, and along the hall. It was worse than the first floor. Chunks of plaster had fallen onto the bare wooden floor from the ceiling. A terrible stench arose from somewhere. The toilets apparently didn't work.

I tried the third floor and found more of the same. Finally, I heard a TV behind one door, and knocked on it. There was no answer, except that the TV stopped playing. I knocked again.

"Hello?"

After a few minutes, the door opened a crack, and an eye in a wrinkled, grizzled face peered fearfully out.

"I'm trying," said a trembly voice.

"What?"

"I'm trying, but I can't find no place to go."

"Excuse me," I told the eye. "I'm looking for Wanda Wrightson."

The door opened a little more then, and I was able to make out an elderly, white-haired woman wrapped in a dirty blue shawl.

"Wanda?" she croaked uncertainly.

"She used to live here."

"What's she look like?"

"Well . . . kind of flashy. Dark hair. She's a hooker."

"A what?" The old woman frowned uncertainly.

"A streetwalker."

"Oh, them! Aren't they awful, though!" She tisk-tisked, and muttered something through the crack of the door. "They moved them in and dopers too. Everything's going."

The old woman seemed disoriented and vague. Beyond her, I could see her apartment was dimly lit and almost barren of furniture.

"She probably got evicted," she said. "They're throwing us all out."

"Who?"

"The landlord. They said we got to move."

I wasn't able to ask her any more, however, because a look of terror came over her face and the door creaked shut in my face. I realized there was another presence in the battered corridor. I turned and it was the surly looking building super.

"Whata you want?" he said threateningly.

"I told you. Wanda Wrightson."

"And I told you she don't live here. You got no right in here."

I had the feeling he would not hesitate to throw me out. I felt myself wishing I had Bike O'Malley with me, or that I was as large as Bike.

"Out," he growled.

I walked past him, waiting for a shove or a punch, and went back down the swaying staircase. He clumped down behind me and followed me to the front door. I went out, and when I glanced back he was standing in the door like a guard.

I walked along the street, wondering if I could find the other hooker, the one who lived around on Second Avenue. There were more battered, wounded buildings along the street, and when I got around onto Second Avenue the building where Cecelia was supposed to live was like the one where Wanda no longer lived. Windows boarded up. A demolished entrance.

I kept going around the block, circling to come back on the next side street to Third Avenue again, and by now I saw what I hadn't realized before. The entire block was in a state of demolition or flight.

By the time I got back to Kelly's, I could see that the

New Dublin Inne was about the only sound structure still occupied in the whole block.

And now, "anonymous" had engineered two prostitution arrests in Kelly's bar, which was enough to put Timmy Kelly's palce in jeopardy.

25

I DIDN'T GET a chance to talk to Timmy before the State Liquor Authority hearing the next morning. When I came back from my tour around the block, Little Denny, the bartender, told me Timmy was meeting with his lawyer about the hearing.

So, the next morning Bike O'Malley and I showed up at S.L.A. offices at 250 Broadway down across from City Hall.

Timmy was dressed in his church usher suit again, and looked both vulnerable and disgusted. Bike and I were shamefaced. Only the lawyer seemed ready for it.

We rode up in an elevator and stood in a corridor outside the S.L.A. hearing room while Timmy's lawyer, Thornton, went inside and found out what would happen.

We stood there smoking, looking at each other and then looking away, and trying to think of what to say. Then I saw McGuire of Public Morals, and the other cop. They stood away from us down the corridor.

A few minutes later, I noticed another familiar figure. Large and bony faced, but dressed up in a Sears, Roebuck suit with his hair slicked back as though he were going to a funeral. The burly super I had had the run-in with in the falling-down building down the block from Kelly's. When he saw me, he looked away.

Before I could figure out what he was doing there, Thornton, the lawyer, came out and told us we should go into the hearing room. There was the S.L.A. hearing officer on an upraised platform, with a clerk beside him, and standing at a table in front of him was the S.L.A. counsel. We slid into seats and waited.

When the case against the New Dublin Inne was called, the Public Morals Squad cops both testified about busting the two hookers in the place. Both hookers had long records for prostitution.

Thornton the lawyer, short and trim with sandy hair and a three-piece suit, strutted up to the hearing officer and let fly Timmy's defense.

"My client disclaims any knowledge of these women," he declared. "Mr. Kelly is a man of solid reputation both in business and in the community, and would not knowingly allow women of this sort to frequent his place of business."

The hearing officer listened and nodded wisely, and then whispered to the clerk. The clerk whispered to the S.L.A. counsel.

"Mr. Skillman?" the counsel said, looking out over the room.

"Here. Yes, Sir." And who stood up but the super in the Sears, Roebuck suit and the slicked-back hair.

"Will you come up, please?"

Mr. Skillman walked to the front of the hearing room, was sworn in by the clerk, and sat down to testify.

"Mr. Skillman, do you live in the vicinity of the New Dublin Inne?" the counsel asked him.

"Yes, Sir. Several doors away."

"What is your occupation?"

"I'm the super . . . the building superintendent there."

Thornton the lawyer leaned over to Timmy. "What's this?" he asked. Timmy shrugged.

I was going to fill in the lawyer on what I knew, but the counsel was questioning Mr. Skillman again.

"You are a member of a block association in your block, are you not?" asked the counsel.

"I'm the president of the Neighborhood Improvement Association."

I had to blink at that one. Neighborhood Improvement Association? Why, the guy presided over a shambles of a place that was all but deserted.

"In your capacity as block association president, Mr. Skillman, have you had occasion to notice the New Dublin Inne?"

"Yes, Sir," said the excellent Mr. Skillman, and his face became self-righteous. "It's the worst gin mill on the block."

"Objection," burst from our Thornton the lawyer, who had recovered himself enough to stand up and pay attention.

"All right, all right," said the hearing officer up on his pedestal. He looked at the lawyer wearily. "There's no jury here, Mr. Thornton. This is all informal. The witness will refrain from offering unsolicited opinions."

"The New Dublin Inne has been located at the same corner for upwards of fifty years," Thornton went on. "It has never before had as much as one alleged violation."

"Yes, Counselor," said the officer.

"And it is the *only* licensed bar in the block."

"Can we get on?" the officer said with annoyance.

"Now, then," the S.L.A. lawyer said. "Mr. Skillman, have you lodged formal complaints against the New Dublin Inne?"

"Yes, Sir," said the super.

Timmy and I exchanged glances. Here was our "anonymous" caller.

"What form did they take?"

"Huh?"

"With whom did you lodge your complaints against the New Dublin Inne?" the counsel repeated.

"I told the cops about it," said Skillman. "I told them there were hookers working outa there."

"And how did you know this?"

Well, said Mr. Skillman, he had walked by and had seen the trollops prancing up and down on the corner. He had looked inside, and gone inside, as well, and had satisfied himself that the New Dublin Inne was, in fact, an occasion of sin.

"There were underage kids getting served in there, too," he added.

"Objection! There is no alleged violation charging the serving of minors." From Thornton.

"Sustained," said the hearing officer. "Stick to the allegations, please."

Mr. Skillman the righteous superintendent explained that his tenants were outraged at the presence of hookers in the neighborhood, and he had felt it was his duty as a citizen to do something about it.

I sat there squirming, wishing I were a lawyer so I could ask Mr. Skillman a few questions. But I had to be satisfied to huddle with Thornton during a brief pause in the proceedings. I told him about Skillman.

"Mr. Skillman," Thornton attacked when things resumed, "isn't it a fact that one of the women arrested for soliciting lives in your building?"

And that's when a tall, blond man who looked a little like Dave DeBuschere, the old Knicks basketball forward, strode up to the hearing officer's dais.

"Mr. Duncan, I am Marvin McQuade of McQuade, Weiss and Tyler, the lawyer for the Neighborhood Improvement Association, and if Mr. Skillman is going to be cross-examined, I wish to represent him."

"Yes, yes, let's move on," said the hearing officer.

Well! So the falling down rattrap was not only headquarters for the Neighborhood Improvement Association, but had a lawyer as well.

156

"You may answer the question," the S.L.A. counsel told Skillman, meaning the one about the hooker living in his building.

"No, of course no hookers live in my building," said Skillman, darting a black look at me in the seats.

Then Thornton introduced the police arrest form, which said Wanda Wrightson gave her address as his building.

"I don't care. She don't live there," he growled.

Marvin McQuade, the Neighborhood Improvement lawyer, asked to see the arrest report. He examined it minutely, as lawyers will, and then asked the hearing officer if he could direct a question to Detective McGuire of the Public Morals Squad, who was sitting in the spectators' seats.

"Yes, yes," the officer snapped, "Officer McGuire, you may answer from there. You're still under oath."

Marvin McQuade had to pace back and forth once first, to get into the mood, apparently. Then he looked at McGuire.

"Officer McGuire, isn't is a fact that Wanda Wrightson has been arrested many times, and has given many addresses?"

"Yes, Sir," answered the Public Morals cop.

"Are you prepared to say that she lived in the building mentioned here?"

"No, Sir, I wouldn't swear where she lives."

"This is just the latest address she used, is that right?"

"Yes, Sir."

A nice performance, I had to admit. But McQuade wasn't finished, not by a long shot. Turning to Skillman, he asked, "Mr. Skillman, do you have any knowledge of this Wrightson woman who it is alleged lived in your building?"

"No, Sir." he said, and a sly smile played over his

bony mug. "Unless she brought her customers into the building from Kelly's when I wasn't lookin'."

"Objection!" Thornton was still on the job.

"Sustained," said the hearing officer.

"Now, Mr. Skillman," McQuade went on, pacing with his long legs again, "why did you say she brought her customers into your building?"

"Because," declared Skillman, sitting forward now, "one of the guys who hangs around Kelly's came into the building looking for her."

I froze at that.

"Which person do you mean?" asked McQuade with a show of innocence.

"There he is right there, sitting with Mr. Kelly." And Skillman leaned forward to point me out. It was too late to slide under the chair.

Thornton gaped at me, then at McQuade, and then at Skillman, and nothing came out of his mouth.

"May we have the gentleman stand and identify himself?" asked the impudent Neighborhood Improvement lawyer.

I sat there like a stone, a red-faced and thoroughly disgusted stone.

"The gentleman will stand and identify himself," said the hearing officer, peering out over the seats.

I stood up. "Edward Fitzgerald." I gave the hearing officer a look and added, "New York *Daily Press*."

The hearing officer's head bobbed a little, and he took another look at me.

But McQuade, the towering attorney, claimed the hearing officer's attention, and mine, too, by striding back and forth and pointing a long arm and a long finger at me, as though I were the town miscreant held fast in the public stocks in old New Amsterdam.

"Did you ever see this man in your building?" he

asked of Skillman, still leveling that accusing pointed finger at me.

"Yeah. He came over one day looking for Wanda. I told him we got no hookers here. He should go to Kelly's if that's what he wants."

Thornton was holding his mouth by now, and I still stood there, frozen, my head in the stock, wondering what was going on.

McQuade soon showed me. He waved that imperious arm at McGuire again. "Officer McGuire, it was Mr. Fitzgerald that Wanda made a date with in Kelly's the day you arrested her, was it not?"

"Date?" popped out of me.

"Yes, Sir," said McGuire the detective, and I think he smiled a little.

"Wait a minute," I started.

"I'm through with you. You may sit down," McQuade tossed at me, turning his back and dismissing me as being a disembowled thing of no further use except to be thrown to the dogs.

It's marvelous the way lawyers command a courtroom, or even an informal hearing room, with their peremptory manner, and it's a shameful admission that I let him get away with it, sinking slowly back into my seat.

McQuade kept going, though, turning to face the heavy-jawed super and striking a prosecutorial pose with his arms folded across his chest.

"And is that why you lodged a complaint, Mr. Skillman? Because the hooker trade from Kelly's was threatening to taint your building?"

"Yeah. That's right," grinned the lying thug.

And there you have it. McQuade and Skillman had performed a dazzling feat of reversal. It was not Wanda Wrightson the fresh-mouthed hooker who had been sallying forth from Skillman's building to ply her trade at

Kelly's. It was Kelly's that was providing a haven for prostitutes who then took their benighted johns to Skillman's building and disgraced the outraged tenants there.

Well, Thornton the three-piece suit finally found his voice again, and gave a pretty good ranting defense, insisting that it was all nonsense.

"These crumbling buildings of which Mr. Skillman is one of the managers are the only eyesores or gathering places for undesirables in the block," he yelled.

But it didn't help. There had been two documented prostitution arrests in the New Dublin Inne, and the S.L.A. must deal with them.

That was bad enough, but then came the real kicker.

The lanky McQuade got up again and identified himself as the legal representative of the owner of several buildings in the block.

"I also represent the owner of the property on which the New Dublin Inne is situated," he said.

I looked at Timmy. Timmy looked at Thornton the lawyer. Thornton looked back at us.

"Now that these violations have come to our attention," McQuade galloped on, "my client moves for the eviction of the leaseholder, Mr. Kelly."

"Jesus, Mary, and Joseph!" Timmy Kelly was white as blank paper.

26

AFTERWARD, WE ALL stumbled out into the corridor in a state of shock. All except McQuade, who looked pleased as a London barrister who had just gotten Jack the Ripper acquitted.

McQuade hadn't succeeded in getting Timmy summarily tossed out, but the New Dublin Inne was under suspension for thirty days. Any further arrests and he would be forcibly retired to Florida and the pelicans. And with the block full of hookers and derelicts, the chance for more arrests was good to inevitable.

"That McQuade," I asked Timmy, "is he the landlord's lawyer who came around and tried to buy up your lease?"

"Naw, never saw him before. It was some other guy. Brennan . . . Brennan something. But he was from that same firm he mentioned . . . McQuade and somebody. I remember that now."

At which point the towering Marvin McQuade walked out and joined us.

"Who is this bunch that wants me out?" Timmy demanded of the lanky attorney. "This Limited Improvement gang?"

"Your landlord. The Limited Improvement Development Corporation," smiled McQuade unctuously.

"And who the devil is that?"

"I represent them," he said.

"What about that other squirt who came around . . . Brennan?"

"Yes. He's with our firm."

"And why do they want me out? Another damned McDonald's?"

McQuade surveyed Timmy and me and Thornton a moment.

"My client does not want illegal activity on property he owns," said McQuade. "It's that simple."

"Simple, huh?" spat Timmy. "Oh, it's simple enough. You tried to buy me out, then you sent in a plague of inspectors on me!"

"We're interested parties," the smoothie smiled.

Thornton pushed his way in. "You and that super of yours sent those girls in there," he howled. "That's harrassment!"

"You heard the testimony," snapped McQuade. "The girls came from your saloon to our buildings."

"You want my corner!" Timmy declared flatly.

"My client is interested in acquiring your lease," McQuade smiled. "We are prepared to buy it up."

"I got ten years left!" said Timmy. "I ain't going nowhere."

"That, of course, is your privilege," the tall lawyer said, not jovially. "If you change your mind . . . my card."

And Timmy was left with a lawyer's card in his hand as McQuade strode down the corridor to the elevators. Only then did I realize that the building super had already vanished.

We walked outside onto Broadway, and I was spinning with the crazy turn of events. Timmy Kelly was in a squeeze play. Some real estate developer hiding behind McQuade and the euphonious name Limited Improvement Development Corporation had bought up the land under Timmy's bar and meant to force him out, lease or no lease. They had made offers to buy him out, and now were using other methods.

"I'll file a harrassment action," Thornton the lawyer was telling Timmy calmly. "You have a valid lease. There's nothing to worry about."

"Jesus," said Timmy.

Bike O'Malley stood there silently, and when he glanced at me I could tell he needed a drink.

I slid off across Broadway, my mind on its own scent. Through City Hall Park, past the seated statue of Horace Greeley looking west, and to the Surrogate Court building on Chambers Street across from the huge, white Municipal Building.

You go up to Room 203 to the office of the Register of Deeds and ask a clerk for help.

"Do you know the block number?" he asked me.

"Block number?"

"All right," he said, leaning on the long counter. "Go into the plate room and find the location."

"Plate room?"

He pointed to a doorway. "Right through there."

The plate room is a huge expanse filled with big, square plate-glass leaves that swing open like the pages of a gigantic book. On each plate behind glass doors are sections of the city in map form, block by block. Each block is numbered, and each lot is, also. You turn the big, glass pages until you find the location you want. And there it was—the block on which the New Dublin Inne was located.

I jotted down the block number and then the lot number for each property in the block—Timmy's block—and took it to the clerk again. In a moment, he had punched the numbers into a computer and had it for me.

"Yes, well, these properties are owned by the Limited Improvement Development Corporation," he said.

"What . . . all of them?"

"That's what it shows. Yes."

I stood there like a rock. The entire block had been bought up by Limited Improvement Development Corporation. I walked downstairs into the sprawling, marble nave of the Surrogate Court building, which is a gaudy, old museum of a place, and it was just what I had suspected all along. It could mean only one thing. A developer planned to put up a building on that block, and only Timmy's saloon stood in his way. That, a fifteen-year lease, and Timmy Kelly's Irish stubbornness.

But who was the Limited Improvement Development Corporation?

When I got to the office, Ironhead Matthews was wearing his Missing Person's face. The missing person, of couse, was me.

"Fitzgerald," he said, looking exasperatedly at me, "you're supposed to report for work here in the morning. But where do you go?"

"Well, see—"

"You come here and get an assignment, and *then* you go out, understand?"

"Sure, Ironhead, but—"

"But you don't do that. You go on an assignment first, and *then* you show up here any time you goddam please!"

"But—"

"Now, if it isn't a state secret, would you like to tell your city editor just where in the geographical goddam hell you've been?"

"At the Register of Deeds office."

Ironhead glared at me for a second, and then paused to relight his revoltingly slimy cigar. He puffed and chewed on it for a millennium, all the while searching my face hopefully.

"About buildings?" he asked.

"Yes."

He almost smiled at that. "What have you come up with?"

"It was because of that hooker," I explained.

"Hooker?"

"The one that picked me up in Timmy's."

"Wait a minute!" Ironhead snapped, holding up a hand like a school crossing guard. "Before you give me another one of your convoluted litanies, tell me one simple thing."

"What's that?"

"Is there a story in it about buildings?" It was logical enough.

"Well, in a way."

"Would you be kind enough to tell me in what way?"

"As soon as I can figure it out."

I was woefully incorrect about *that*, Ironhead said. Because I seemed to always figure stories out after the circle replate, or two weeks after the story was dead as Kelsey's you-know-what, and it was time I realized that the job of a *Daily Press* reporter was to find stories and actually write them so they could be for chrissake *printed* and *read* and that would help sell newspapers!

Had I any conception that while I was out stumbling through the corridors of the Register of Deeds that a hot story was awaiting me at the city desk? Did I care enough to call in and find out that one Colin Christopher had won $3 million in the State Lottery and that I was supposed to be interviewing him? Did I have the brains of a gnat? Did I want to be assigned as the lobster obit writer?

And so I was banished to my desk, given the home phone number of Colin Christopher the sudden millionaire, and told to do a telephone interview with him. Then I would return to the Romance of Buildings!

Colin Christopher told me that he was "never so

surprised in his life," and that "this won't change him," and that "God's hand" and his wife's hand picked the numbers, and that "this is the greatest country in the world."

After I wrote that hot story, I sat back and lit a Tiparillo, trying to give some thought to skyscrapers. But I kept thinking of falling-down tenements and wondering who had bought them up.

Then I spotted the messages from Archer Whitney on my desk, including the tantalizing one saying we had "both been right." I still didn't know what that meant.

I called Whitney again, but he still wasn't in his office.

That night at home, I slipped into the bathtub with Marcus Aurelius and sought some of my ancient sage's wisdom.

"Do not disturb yourself by thinking of the whole of your life," he declaimed. "Let not your thoughts at once embrace all the various troubles which you may expect to befall you. But on every occasion ask yourself, 'What is there in this which is intolerable and past bearing?' Remember that neither the future nor the past pains you, but only the present. But this is reduced to very little, if you only circumscribe it, and scold yourself if you are unable to bear even this."

Meditations went sailing into the corner, and I sank down into the water of the bathtub.

Maybe only the present pained Marcus, but I saw thumbscrews in the past and future as well. I didn't want to see anybody. I didn't want to go anywhere. I had wanted to slip into the pages of *Meditations* and join Marcus's legions at Caruntum fighting the Marcomanni on the Danube. At least that would be clear-cut; the pilium against the spears of the German tribes. But I was fighting rooks and knights that kept transforming themselves into windmills as though the vile Enchanter that bedeviled Don Quixote de la Mancha was also on my case. All right, I know I sound like a lunatic. Don't even ask me.

What was bothering me? Timmy's problems, which I had helped cause, to be sure. But there was something more. I thought I had found peace watching the Pleiades floating across the Massachusetts sky, but here was the soothing serenity of Marcus Aurelius causing me agitation, urging me to "circumscribe" my problems.

I got out of the bathtub, lit a Tiparillo, and realized what it was. That Morse code dat-dit-dat Archer Whitney had left me.

"We were both right."

I had never found out what he meant. Maybe he hadn't gotten to work today. Maybe he had spent the weekend at Turley's making wet Olympic logo rings on the bar with martini glasses. Maybe he was home with a monumental hangover. I got his home number from the phone book and tried him there. Finally, an answer.

"Hello?"

"Arch?"

"Who's calling?"

"Fitzgerald. Who's this?"

"Just a moment."

There was a clunk of the phone being put down, and then somebody else picked it up, and spoke.

"Fitzgerald the reporter?" somebody wanted to know.

"Yeah."

I realized who it was. Detective Messina of the bent nose.

"Messina? What are you doing there?"

"Why are you calling?" He came right back at me.

"I'm trying to reach Archer Whitney."

"About what?"

"About . . . it's complicated. What's the big song and dance, anyway. Have you arrested him or something? Can I talk to him?"

"You can, but you won't get an answer."

27

I DROVE UP to Archer Whitney's apartment on the Upper West Side and found it swarming with cops. A foul-tempered Detective Messina was in charge, and his scowl went into a sulky pout when he saw me. He turned and walked away when I entered. I followed him.

"Somebody got Archer Whitney?" I asked idiotically.

Messina humphed something that I took to mean "yes."

"Do you know who shot him?" I tried again.

Detective Messina finally turned on me. He glared silently for a moment, his lips pursed, and then said, "How do you know he was shot?"

"What?"

"How did you happen to call here?"

"Well . . ."

"How is it that every time there's a murder in this screwy case, you show up?"

"I'm covering the story."

"Story! Goddamit, this isn't a story! It's a murder case!" He stalked away.

Whitney's apartment was basically one big room, with a sort of floor built halfway up across one end to create a bedroom on a balcony overhead, and a kitchen nook under it. There was a small bar and three bar stools at the kitchen nook.

Whitney's body lay sprawled on the floor in front of the bar, covered with a blanket. He apparently had been having a drink with someone at the bar when it happened. A tumbler with his fingerprints on it was found on the floor near the body. Another tumbler on the bar had been wiped clean.

Messina told me the building super had heard music playing from Whitney's apartment every time he passed by during the weekend. When he still heard the music playing Monday afternoon, he had knocked and then entered the apartment. He found Whitney dead of a gunshot wound of the chest. Apparently, Whitney had been dead since Friday evening sometime.

"What do you know about this?" Messina demanded.

"Me? What would I know?" I answered defensively.

"I don't know, Fitzgerald. I can't figure you out a damn bit. You run around bitching up my witnesses. You help my suspect. You get to every damned dead body before I do. Where were you this weekend?"

"Weekend?"

"Yeah."

"Uh . . . with a girl."

"Figures."

I didn't want to say that the girl was Kerry Burke, the witness he complained I had been "bitching up."

"You're not thinking of *me* as a suspect are you?" I asked, confusedly.

"Why not? Everywhere I go, you turn up."

"But, for chrissake, Messina, I'm trying to help."

Messina seemed to have something in his throat because he started coughing and then sneezing.

"Who sent you to Squeaky Duffy's the night he got it?" he wanted to know.

"Skates Stern."

"Humph," muttered Messina. "Skates again."

"You mean he got Whitney, too?"

Messina stalked away, and I followed. "He made bail again?"

170

Silence.

"Well?"

"Goddamit, he's still in the Tombs."

"What?" Messina's scowl was etched in metal. And then I realized why he was so upset.

"Then Skates couldn't have done it," I said.

"Shit." Messina.

"No, it's somebody else, isn't it?" I pressed him. "The same guy who got James Kelly and Duffy. You've got the wrong guy, haven't you?"

Messina turned on me in a foul temper. "Why did you call here tonight?"

"Oh, yeah," I said. "I was going to tell you. Whitney was checking out something for me."

"What?"

"I don't know."

Messina turned around and shook his head. I heard his breath come out. He sank into a small sofa, and I sat across from him in a chair.

"He was checking something out for you, but you don't know what it was?" He sounded very tired.

I explained that I had asked Whitney about James's $350,000 commission, and thought he was looking into it.

"What about the commission?" he asked.

"How could James get a commission when he didn't have a real estate license? And the building was sold before he started working there."

Messina was annoyed. "I checked that out," he said. "His boss, Magen, was in on that sale, and he has a license. And James had come to Magen with a lead on that deal before he started working there. That's how he got the job. It's all legal and aboveboard."

"Oh," I said, deflated. I had felt sure that's what Whitney had been looking into. And something still bothered me about it, although I couldn't put my finger on it.

"Any leads here?" I asked.

Messina grunted negatively.

"No fingerprints, huh?" I said.

"No," snapped Messina. "No prints, no gun, nothing."

It was all becoming too much for me, this ordinary murder that kept spreading around New York. Messina was still in a brown study, walking around the apartment.

"No prints at Duffy's, either," he said. "No gun there, either. Nothing."

"How about at James's place?" I asked. "Any prints there?"

"Yeah. James's. On the phone."

"Oh."

Messina looked sunk and discouraged.

"Maybe we ought to work together," I suggested feebly, and got a look that would have demolished Rockefeller Center.

"You're not really building a case against me?" I tried again.

Messina just watched me.

I pointed out that somebody had tried to make me one of the victims, too. Besides, what reason would I have?

"Just don't give me one," he warned.

I left, realizing that the whole James Kelly case was wide open again. My instinct about Skates might have been right, after all. Something Messina had said played through my mind.

James's fingerprints on the phone.

James had been on the phone talking to Kerry Burke when he was shot, she said. After being hit three times from a nine millimeter, James had hung up the phone?

28

I DROVE BACK to my place in something of a daze and called Rick Massilli at the city desk to fill him in on the latest.

"What?" said Massilli. "You found another one?"

"I didn't exactly find him."

"What the hell is this, Fitz?" he said. "I thought you were working days."

"I am."

"Then how come you keep calling me on the nightside with all these damned stiffs?"

After a certain amount of this ragging, I finally turned the story over to a rewrite man. When I hung up, I suddenly thought of the effect this would have on Kerry Burke. She was about ready to jump out of her skin as it was. I glanced at the clock. It was after midnight, but I decided to call her anyway.

"Hello?"

"Kerry, it's Fitz."

"Hi," she said sleepily.

"Listen, I don't know how to tell you this. It's about Archer."

I could sense a reaction. I imagined her eyes opening wide. She was hanging on my words.

"Oh, God," she gasped.

"I'm sorry."

"He's not . . ."

"Somebody shot him."

Kerry was moaning, keening, as though she couldn't speak. "It isn't worth it," she finally whimpered.

"I didn't want you to read it in the paper," I said.

"Thanks."

"Are you all right?"

"I don't know, Fitz. It's all so awful. Is it ever going to stop?"

"It will stop," I assured her. "When it gets this bad, something usually cracks."

That seemed to quiet her. "What . . . why?" she gulped.

"Because too much has happened now. It's going to start adding up. It has to."

I wasn't sure I really believed that, but I wanted to calm her down.

"What happened with . . . with Arch?" she said then.

"I don't know. He was looking into the money James was paid. He must have found something out."

"But what?"

"I don't know. He left me a message that we were both right about it, but I can't figure out what he meant. Are you going to be all right?"

"I guess so," she murmured uncertainly.

"You want me to come over?"

"No, I'm all right."

"Lunch tomorrow?"

"Okay . . . yes."

"About one o'clock . . . at that teahouse?"

"All right."

After I hung up, I tried to add things up myself. Two salesmen from Magen & Burke, and a small-fry loan shark in Brooklyn. And Skates Stern. Let us not forget him. How did they add up? It was simple enough. They didn't. The chain that linked them together was still missing, or at least I couldn't see it. Maybe it was too close to me, such as wound around my neck like the albatross in the "Rime of the Ancient Mariner."

I didn't sleep much that night. I kept hearing Arch's message, "We were both right," drip, drip, dripping on me like a Chinese water torture. Right about what?

"He didn't sell a birdhouse," Arch had said. He was right about that?

"I know he was paid that commission," I had told him. Was I right about that, too?

Then Fu Manchu Messina let fall a drop. "He was paid the commission. So what?"

The drops kept falling onto my forehead until I finally slid off up the Yangtze River and was tormented all night by prancing, gamboling dragons.

The next morning when I got to the city room, I checked with Detective Messina and, as I had told Kerry, things were starting to unravel.

"Now, listen, I don't want this printed yet," said Messina. "Okay?"

"What is it?"

"I asked . . . okay?"

"All right." The damned tight-lipped dick!

"I just got the report back from ballistics. The gun that killed Archer Whitney is the same one that killed Sylvester Duffy."

"You're sure?"

"No! I made it up! Yes, goddamit, I'm sure."

"What do you make of it?"

"I don't know, yet. I'm only telling you this to keep you up to date so you won't go careening around town getting into more trouble. Now, stay out of it."

"But—"

"But what?"

"Dammit, Messina, somebody tried to put a hole in my ear, too, you know. I'm not some disinterested bystander."

"Shit."

"What?"

"You heard me." And he was gone.

I told Jim Owens I was going downtown to check on a building, and then hurried out before he or Ironhead could ask me what building. I was going to check on one, all right—the Bayton Building. Because I couldn't let go of the idea that the reason things didn't add up was simply because they *did* add up. In particular, James making that fat commission by selling the Bayton Building. If James had made that money honestly on a legitimate deal, then I had no handle on anything. But I didn't believe it. There had to be something about it that wasn't kosher.

Back down the FDR Drive to Foley Square, where I parked behind Police Headquarters and walked through St. Andrews Plaza past the Municipal Building to Surrogate Court.

Upstairs to Room 203 again, and then into the plate room where I found the block and lot number for the Bayton Building. Back out to the clerk, and asked him to punch the information into his computer.

"Yes, well, this property changed hands March 4th," he said. "Let's see . . . Littlefield and Downs are the new title holders." He gave me their address on Broad Street.

I walked downstairs into the sprawling, marble nave of the Surrogate Court building and found a pay phone.

"Littlefield and Downs," came an efficient voice when I called the firm.

"Mr. Littlefield?"

"I'm sorry, Mr. Littlefield is out."

"Mr. Downs?"

"I'm sorry."

"Who can I speak to about a building your firm recently bought?"

A pause. "Who's calling, please?"

I invented fast. "The city tax department. We need some information for our files."

In a moment I was connected to a Mr. Mallon, who informed me rapidly that the sale was a routine transaction.

"Yes, I know," I said. "But we need to know who handled the sale. We don't show any payment of the city's transfer tax on this transaction."

Mr. Mallon became extremely cooperative. "Well, I handled it for Littlefield and Downs, and I assure you—"

"And how about for Magen & Burke?"

"Shouldn't you ask them, Mr. . . . ?"

"Fitzgerald. You see, Mr. Mallon, they're the ones we're investigating. Not you."

"Oh!" A high gasp of relief that slid down into a comfortable conclusion. "That's good. What kind of tax are you looking into?" he said then, apparently wondering at my rather slipshod questioning.

"It's quite complicated," I said as calmly as I could. "City income tax, transfer tax, and the IRS has queried us."

"IRS? Mr. Fitzgerald, all I know is that I handled it for Littlefield and Downs, and Mr. Magen handled it for them."

"Yes, of course. And what was the sale price?"

"Why, uh . . . twelve-eight, as I recall."

"Twelve-eight? Twelve million, eight hundred thousand?"

"Yes."

I tried to keep the gasp out of my voice. "And what's the commission on a sale like that?"

Mr. Mallon paused a moment. "Why, the usual commission."

"Oh. The usual commission." I tried to pretend I was thinking that over. "Not higher?"

"No. Six percent. Standard. Why?"

"Well, we need to know if a Mr. James Kelly was paid a commission on this transaction."

"Kelly?"

"We're informed that he was the selling agent."

"Kelly?" Mallon said again. "Well, no, there was no Kelly."

Ha! I thought, and wished I could reach through the phone and give him a nice kiss.

"No Kelly?" I pressed him. "You're sure no commission was paid to a James Kelly on this deal?" Hope rose in me. Magen said James was paid that money for the Bayton deal, and here was somebody telling me it wasn't so. Here was the beginning of the trail of the hanky-panky.

Even as I rolled this hopeful nugget around in my head, I realized that Mallon had fallen silent.

"Uh, you're not bringing us into this, are you?" he finally spoke again.

"Not unless it becomes necessary," I told him, trying to sound reasonable and yet severe at the same time. "But if Kelly was paid a commisson, and that information is withheld . . . "

"But you see, sir, he could have been, and we wouldn't know it," said Mallon, his voice rising.

"What do you mean?" I asked, not liking what I was hearing.

"What Mr. Magen did with his commission is up to him. He could have paid this Kelly a finder's fee or whatever. It has nothing to do with us."

"But he wasn't part of the deal, as far as you know? It was only you and Konrad Magen?"

"Yes. And the lawyers, of course."

"Lawyers? What lawyers?"

178

"Well, Holdman and Womack for us. And I believe they were represented by Mr. McQuade."

"McQuade? Marvin McQuade?" The lanky basketball form popped into my mind.

"Yes."

McQuade and Magen? The combination positively opened doors within doors inside my echoing brain.

"Was Magen operating under the name of Limited Improvement Development Corporation?" I asked him.

"No, no. As Magen & Burke."

"Thanks, Mr. Mallon," I told him, and hung up.

I walked out of Surrogate Court in something of a daze. The soaring figures left me in confusion because, like Disraeli, I know nothing of finance. Still, I could figure out that a six percent commission on $12.8 million was $768,000. If James had shared equally in that commission, he would have gotten $384,000.

Driving uptown to Madam Charriere's yellow teahouse, I was disgusted and frustrated. I kept trying to prove that James Kelly had come by that money in some crooked way, and all I succeeded in doing was finding out that he seemed to have made it legitimately.

Kerry was waiting for me at her table by the window, and her presence still lighted up the place, despite the glum look on her lovely face.

After the brown teapots came, I reached across the table and held her hand.

"How're you doing, kid?" I asked her.

"I don't know, Fitz," she murmured, "I just don't know. Did you find out anything?"

I sighed and sipped my tea. "Yeah. It looks like James could have been paid in that Bayton deal."

"But I told you that," she said, leaning across the table.

"I know."

"In fact, I looked into it some more," she went on,

"and it wasn't a regular commission. It was partly a bonus and partly a finder's fee. It's done all the time."

"Terrific."

James Kelly worked at Magen & Burke from about April or May until June and made $350,000 and there was nothing unusual about it? As the water in my cup clouded with the spreading dark tea color, I felt the same dark cloud spreading over me.

29

I TRIED TO go look at some buildings for the series that afternoon, but it was hopeless. The only building I could think of was the Bayton Building. Finally, I drove down to Kelly's with the idea of sitting over a stein of Harp beer to ponder it out. But of course, Kelly's was shuttered—under that thirty-day S.L.A. suspension.

In the side street running from Third to Second avenues, I saw a mass of equipment, including an immense crane with a dangling wrecker's ball on a cable. More of the old buildings were coming down, or were already down. With Timmy's place closed up, the whole block was in a deserted state.

I wandered across Third Avenue into another old bar—McAnn's—and ordered a beer. I sat there staring into it, no longer cloudy like the tea, but still obscured with foam. From where I sat I could see Timmy's across the street, and also some of the buildings along the side street, and the demolition crews.

And who did I see getting out of a car but Konrad Magen. He walked up the steps into the building where Wanda Wrightson had supposedly lived, and where Skillman the super held sway, the gentleman of the dazzling testimony. It looked like that particular tenement was being torn down now.

Konrad Magen. He floated about in the background of everything. He's in on the Bayton deal and so is that lawyer, Marvin McQuade. McQuade and his firm are in

181

on the buying up of buildings in Timmy's block, and now here's Magen in the same block.

And finally, it began to penetrate my foggy brain.

I left the glass of beer unfinished on the bar, went to my Mustang, and drove downtown to the Manhattan State Supreme Court building at Foley Square. I had at last realized where to find what I needed to know.

I parked behind Police Headquarters in the NYP zone, and walked over to the Supreme Court, up the wide, stone steps and in under the huge columns across the front.

I had once covered Supreme Court, and got a big hello when I walked into the press room and found Harry Reeves of the *Post,* a jolly leprechaun who had been on that beat forever.

"Fitzboggen!" he chortled. Reeves always called me that because, he explained, "all you Irishers are out of the peat bogs."

"Look, you old fart," I said, "how can I find the names of the people behind a company?"

"What kind of a company? If it's a cat house, I can't help you."

"A corporation. Real estate."

"Okay," he said. "I realize when you covered this building you couldn't even find the men's room. You want to check the business incorporation records in the county clerk's office in the basement."

I walked to the great rotunda and rode the elevator downstairs. Billy, the senior clerk, directed me to the business records room.

"Name of the corporation?" the man at the long counter asked me.

"Limited Improvement Development Corporation," I told him.

He scurried away into the files and brought me back the business incorporation papers.

I looked at the papers and as expected found the name of the attorney, Marvin McQuade. Then, the name of the incorporator.

Paul Dragget.

Dragget . . . Dragget . . . ? The name danced tantalizingly through my mind. Where had I heard it before?

"Excuse me," I asked the clerk, "this name listed as the incorporator . . . does that mean he owns the corporation?"

The clerk took the papers and looked them over. "At least one officer of the corporation has to put his name down," he said.

"Then there can be others in this corporation?"

"Oh, sure."

"But they don't have to be listed?"

"Nope. Just one."

"How can I find the others?"

"Contact the corporation, I guess. Ask the lawyer."

Yes. Marvin McQuade.

"Thanks," I told the clerk, and gave him the paper back.

Dragget . . . ?

And then it came to me. That day I had called Magen & Burke fishing for anybody who knew James Kelly. The vinyl-covered receptionist had suggested "Mr. Dragget."

So the Limited Improvement Development Corporation was a creature of Magen & Burke, Real Estate Brokers & Managers.

And then, finally, I understood why James had been paid that $350,000 and why he had been killed.

30

OUT OF THE State Supreme Court building and down the wide, Hollywood stone steps into Foley Square, and around to my Mustang parked behind Police Headquarters.

I drove past the sprawling mustard-colored Police Headquarters and went north on Park Row, up through Chatham Square, the crossroads of Chinatown, and on up the street that became the Bowery and then turned into Third Avenue. My mind was spinning in a frenzy.

Buildings! That's what it was about. Or more specifically, one building. The glass-and-chrome scale model of the Magen Building floated into my head, the glistening monument that was to be Konrad Magen's permanent addition to the Big Apple.

Konrad Magen and his ally, Marvin McQuade, had bought up every property in Timmy Kelly's block, using a dummy corporation. Finally, they owned the whole block, but there was Timmy Kelly still in his saloon with ten years to go on a fifteen-year lease, and a load of Irish stubbornness stretching all the way back through his father, Liam, to Dublin.

Timmy wouldn't sell his lease to them, and without that corner property no Magen Building could rise. And then providence and Kerry Burke's beauty delivered into their hands the instrument for solving the problem—James Kelly.

I could hear James now, telling Timmy he "didn't give

a damn" about the saloon. But he had taken over the bar anyway, which is something I had never been able to understand.

But now I did. James Kelly had taken over Timmy's for one reason—to sell it to Magen. The $350,000 he was paid was for Timmy's bar, not for the Bayton Building.

No wonder James had been frantic when Timmy decided not to let him have the place after all. James already had his money; had, in fact, already spent a lot of it.

What had happened? Magen must have asked for his money back, and James didn't have it. So he killed James.

Then, I decided, Magen must have jiggered his books to show that the $350,000 was paid to James for the Bayton Building, because he couldn't afford to be linked to Timmy's bar after James was murdered.

That's what Archer Whitney had wanted to tell me. We were both right! James was paid the money, all right, but for Timmy's lease.

It never fails when you're trying to drive somewhere in a hurry in Manhattan that traffic slows in front of you. Just above Thirty-fourth Street, the cars were halted in all lanes, and I could see blinking yellow and red lights ahead. I inched along in the bumper-to-bumper jam, and it wasn't until I'd gotten just above Thirty-sixth that I realized the clog was caused by fire trucks. And when I got a little closer, I saw the smoke and flames pouring out of Timmy's bar.

The exasperated cop at the corner was waving me on up Third Avenue when I stopped and yelled out the window.

"Fitzgerald, *Daily Press*." I stuck my press card at him and turned into the side street.

"Go on, go on," he shouted.

Into the side street, also choked with police sector

cars, a red fire marshal's car, and those demolition vehicles at the curb topped with a crane and an iron wrecking ball hanging down on a cable. I slid the Mustang into an alley next to Skillman the super's building, which was already in a state of half-collapse.

Squirm out, and dart to the corner.

What a frightful spectacle is a place you know and love under attack from the inside by fire and smoke and from the outside by firemen with axes and thudding streams of water from fire hoses, crumpling the place even as it's supposedly being saved.

I found a fire marshal standing outside in his slicker and fire hat.

"*Daily Press*. What happened?"

"Going pretty good when we got here," he said professionally. "Got too good a start."

"Arson?" I asked.

The fire marshal shuffled his feet. "Under investigation. The fire was going in several places. Suspicious fire, I'd call it."

Watching the New Dublin Inne turning black and crumbling, I felt there was nothing "suspicious" about it. Somebody had set it on fire, and I had a pretty good idea who it must have been.

I looked around but didn't see Timmy. Well, he'd find out soon enough.

I ran back down the side street toward Skillman the super's building.

There he was—on the top step of his half-demolished building, looking at the fire with satisfaction. Then he saw me and disappeared into the building.

In a moment I was at the stoop and dashing up into the building, into the plaster-cracked hallway and to the door marked Super.

I banged on it and screamed: "Skillman!"

No reply.

My shoulder went into the flimsy wooden door and it burst open before me. A shabby apartment in incredible, jumbled disarray, piled with TV sets, furniture, rolled-up rugs. It looked as though Skillman had grabbed furniture from tenants when they were out and dragged it into his room. But there was no surly super in the apartment.

I went back out into the grimy hallway and up the canted staircase, yelling, "Skillman!"

Nothing.

Searching the building, the only thing I found was that it was deserted and practically torn down. The poor old crone who had looked out at me was gone, her apartment door standing open and the place abandoned. Evicted, with everyone else.

I gave up and walked back downstairs and out into the street. Firemen were still pouring streams of water into the shriveling, charred skeleton of the New Dublin Inne.

I walked to my Mustang parked in the alley beside Skillman's dilapidated old tenement, and climbed in. I was trembling with rage and helplessness, and sat for a moment to calm down, lighting a Tiparillo.

I saw it only out of the corner of my eye, a moving image, a slowly swinging cable. A quick, darting glance out the window of the car, and there it was, as in slow motion, the great, round iron wrecking ball on the end of a cable, moving gracefully away in an arc, and then reversing its glide to come back.

And then, a fleeting image, Skillman at the controls of the crane, his face flushed, intent upon his work. A mean, rough face—a face I had once seen for a second staring into my Mustang after he had put a bullet through it.

Like a frozen rabbit in the headlights of an oncoming semitrailer truck, I sat in the Mustang watching the iron ball glide inexorably back in my direction, toward a tottering brick wall on the side of Skillman's tenement.

I was trying to start the car, yet fixed in fascination on the sailing ball as it came gliding back . . . back . . . clump!

Over my head, the crumbly brick wall shuddered at the impact and then gracefully leaned off center, coming down on the top of my Mustang in the alley.

An avalanche of dust and bricks and mortar, and the roof came in on me.

31

I WAS IN a coal mine deep under the earth, choking on dust and trapped in a cave-in. The roof pressed against my head, and I was on the floor of the Mustang, my head thundering with the jolt of the brick avalanche. The pain and the confusion only served to tell me I was still alive. I tried to open the door, but it wouldn't budge, apparently crimped and bent into ripples. My lap was covered with glass from the windshield and the door windows.

Remove the shards of glass gingerly, and squeeze my head toward the door window. Coughing in the dust, rubbing my eyes, trying to see out through the window.

Gradually, I squeezed myself to the window, which was crimped downward in the center, and gasped for air through the opening. I tried to bend the top of the door frame back upward, but it was unyielding. I looked to the other door and found a little more of an opening still in existence.

Wriggling toward the passenger-side door, I finally managed to get my head outside, and then to shimmy through, out of my iron, sea-bottom, mine-shaft prison.

I leaned against the rubble-covered Mustang, gasping, reflecting that the car had been a doomed, dumb thing from the start. The Mustang and I weren't meant to be, it seemed. But Clotho, the Greek Fate who spins our thread of life, apparently was not yet ready to snip my own cord.

I shook my head, trying to clear it, trying to let in air

and light and reason. Because I felt I had to think now, and quickly. Something was prodding me, a voice was calling down a long, murky tunnel, warning me, alerting me.

"Fitz!"

I recognized the voice at once. Kerry Burke!

Because in a rush it all poured over me. The Niagara of tumbling bricks had knocked the entire complex scenario into my fevered mind.

Konrad Magen had bought up Timmy's block for the Magen Building, buying up the lease for the last corner lot—Kelly's bar—from James for $350,000. But when James couldn't deliver the lease after taking the money, Magen had gone to James's apartment to get his money back. The confrontation ended with Magen killing James with his own gun.

Okay. But things went wrong because James called Kerry Burke while Magen was there. Kerry heard them talking, heard the shots, and called the police. Somehow, she had thought it was Skates Stern. It was a perfect mistake for Magen. He let Kerry pin the murder on Skates, keeping himself away from any connection with Timmy's bar.

Enter a bumbling, ink-stained wretch from the *Daily Press*. To wit: me. With Skates's excited assistance, the gun was traced to Squeaky Duffy. Magen couldn't allow Skates to be cleared because he needed a patsy to blame for James's murder.

So Magen—or maybe Skillman—got to Duffy before Skates did.

And what about Archer Whitney? He realized what was going on, that Magen couldn't afford to have it on his books that he paid James Kelly for a lease on the New Dublin Inne. Magen had changed that, so the payment was for the Bayton Building. That's what Whitney wanted to tell me, but Magen or Skillman got to him first.

I stumbled out of the bricks and the alley, back into the side street, still trying to put it together in my ringing skull. Something was still wrong with it, but I couldn't figure it out.

The one fact raging at me was that Kerry Burke was in trouble. Magen knew who was on the phone when he shot James three times. But Kerry didn't know the killer was the wonderful man she trusted and depended upon. And then Kerry started helping me behind Magen's back.

Now that they had tried for the second time to remove me, I had to believe that Kerry was next.

All that for a building? I found myself wondering. But then Konrad Magen's soulful massaging of his glass-and-chrome model in his office floated before me; the Shah Jahan gazing transfixed upon his plans for the Taj Mahal. Yes, Magen wanted it that much.

I walked to the corner where the New Dublin Inne sat shrunken into a black sinkhole of charred lumber and dripping, collapsed walls. Still no Timmy.

I got on a pay phone and called the Nineteenth Precinct squad.

"Detective Messina?"

"Sorry," said a disinterested voice. "Not in."

"Damn."

"What's that?"

"Tell him Fitzgerald called."

"Who?"

"The *Daily Press* reporter."

"Ohhhhhh," came the voice, and it fell off in a long trail at the end, as though to say, "Oh . . . *you*."

I was gradually coming back to some sort of reality, the thudding in my head receding slowly. I walked back down the block to the tenement and the demolition crane and looked around for somebody—anybody. Especially for the bony-jawed mug who had sent that goddam wrecker's ball at me.

A guy wearing a plaid shirt, dust-covered jeans, and a hardhat came sauntering along to the crane, drinking from a cardboard carton.

"Hey," I yelled at him. "Who operates this thing?"

The demolition man gave me a look. "I do. Why?"

"Where've you been?"

"Huh?"

"Just now . . . where's the guy who was running this goddam crane?"

"Who're you?" He had stopped and was giving me a challenging look.

"I'm the guy who was almost killed when that goddam crane knocked that wall down onto my car!"

The demolition man glanced at the wall—or at where the wall had been—and his mouth went open. "Jeez, who done that!"

"That's what I'd like to know."

"Christ," he said, "I been at lunch. Holy shit . . . looka that!"

"Where's Skillman?" I asked.

"He was around before. I dunno."

"How about Mr. Magen?"

"Magen?" he shrugged. Evidently he knew no Mr. Magen.

I walked away, still seething but with no time to stand there dressing the demolition man down. I wanted Skillman.

I hurried to Third Avenue to hail a cab uptown to Magen & Burke on Sixth Avenue, still trying to put together the last pieces of this godawful mess.

Kerry! I had to get uptown before it was too late. I had to hope it wasn't already too late.

I jumped back into the phone booth on the corner and put in a quick call to Kerry at Magen & Burke.

"Kerry?"

"Fitz?"

"Yeah. Listen . . . get out of there, right now!"

"What?"

"Don't argue with me. Get out of there . . . meet me at the tea shop."

Alarm in her voice. "What's the matter?"

"It's all over . . . get out of there, do you hear me?"

"Fitz . . . I've got to talk to you. I don't think you understand . . ."

"Goddamit, I understand . . . !"

"Come on up," she pleaded. "I'll wait for you."

"Kerry!"

But the line was dead.

I jumped in a cab and we headed up Third Avenue. I was cursing myself for not being a more persuasive talker. Konrad Magen had to be putting it all together too, as I was, and he must know by now that Kerry was helping me.

"Hurry, will you?" I told the cabbie.

"You got it," the cabbie snapped back over his shoulder. Of course, you don't really have to tell a New York cabbie to hurry. It's natural for them to swerve along as fast as possible, anyway. But my "hurry" set this driver lurching along like a maniac, throwing me from one side of the back seat to the other. I didn't mind on this occasion.

Up Third Avenue, across Forty-second Street, and then north again up Sixth Avenue to just above Radio City Music Hall. I threw the cabbie some money, bolted from the cab, and dashed in through the Kublai Kahn lobby.

Up in the elevator to the thirty-second floor, and burst through the stylish, swinging glass doors with the fine Bodoni Bold lettering, past the surprised-looking receptionist, who got only halfway to her feet before I was past her.

" . . . can I help you . . . ?"

Faces looking up at me as I darted through the desks and to Kerry's office next to Konrad Magen's. Through the door into Kerry's office.

There she sat, white-faced and trembling, a cigarette shaky in her mouth, her eyes staring at me like saucers.

"Kerry!"

"Eddie . . . "

"Are you all right?"

"Oh, my God . . . "

And then an odd thing. She pressed a button on an intercom and said, "He's here."

The door to Magen's office opened, and in walked Konrad Magen followed by Skillman, the burly super.

I looked at Kerry. Blinking eyes, a trembling mouth. An interrupted half-word " . . . Fitz . . . "

Skillman the super was already stepping behind me to close the door to Kerry's office. Magen closed the door to his. There we stood, all together in the room. And I felt myself sinking into the Irish Sea.

"Well," said Konrad Magen, and out of his pocket he drew an automatic. "You wouldn't quit, would you?"

I looked at Kerry. Then back at Magen. Then at Skillman. And I knew, now, for certain the super's face as the tough-looking mug who had chased me under that garage door and yelled, "Shit." Well, I understood that, anyway. What I didn't understand was the look on Kerry's face.

"I told you to get out of here," I told her uncertainly.

A melicious chuckle from Magen.

Kerry put her face into her hands. And then I knew the impossible.

"No . . . Kerry . . . "

"Eddie, why didn't you let it alone?" she cried. "I tried to tell you . . . . "

"Tell me what?"

I was in a state of depressed confusion. Kerry was in

on this? How? Why? My head swam. I had heard no hints if she had dropped them. How could I? I had seen deeply into those Irish Sea eyes, but never beyond them. When she said she loved me? Maybe so. I had known then it wasn't true. I had never imagined what fear her words masked. For Kerry sat there in terror.

I looked at Magen, who stood there smiling sardonically, evidently enjoying the slow simmering of the smitten reporter.

"You were in on this from the start?" I asked her, still unwilling to believe it.

"No, Eddie . . . no . . . you don't understand."

That was an understatement.

Oddly enough, a wave of cold calculation flooded through me as I stood there. The scales fell from my eyes, at last. Kerry Burke being in on it finally allowed the last pieces of the puzzle to fit together. She hadn't been helping me. She had been helping Magen. That phone call James had made to her when Skates Stern was in James's apartment, for instance.

"You were on the phone with James," I said, "but it wasn't Skates who fired the three shots."

Kerry quietly began to cry. Magen grimaced again.

"She kept James on the phone while you shot him," I said to Magen. He grinned again, maliciously.

"Smart reporter," he sighed. "Still a romantic."

"Okay, Magen," I confessed. "Maybe I can't think clearly about this. But I know what it was about. Timmy's bar. That's why you paid James, and that's why you killed him. Or," I added, sensing the presence of Skillman the thug behind me, "maybe one of your boys did."

"You figured that out, huh?"

"Yeah. And you had it all set up to blame Skates for it, too. What happened? Did Skates just walk in like a patsy at the right time?"

"Just like another person," said Magen.

"Skates was there when somebody called," I said. "So that's it. James didn't call Kerry. She called James, and overheard Skates talking about a bet."

"You're not as dumb as I thought," Magen said sneeringly.

It was all racing through my mind, the whole mass of confused facts playing themselves back and forth again, stopping and then going on, then backwards again.

Skates: "I got my dough and left. Nobody shot nobody."

Kerry: "I heard them talking about a bet, and then three shots."

Messina: "Yeah, there was fingerprints on the phone— James's."

Kerry had called James. Why? To make sure he was home? She overheard Skates there. Then Magen went to James's apartment to get back his $350,000.

"You killed James because he wouldn't give the money back," I ventured.

"Is that what I did?"

"Yeah. And then you blamed it on Skates, because you knew he had just been there. But Skates crossed you up. He told me about buying that gun for James. Then you had to get Duffy. Then I talked to Archer and he was about to blow the whistle. So you got him."

"Impressive," said Magen. "Skill, isn't he bright?"

"Too bright."

I glanced at the burly super. "You came after me when it looked like I was going to clear Skates. You needed that pigeon so nobody would look any deeper into James's murder, so they wouldn't start noticing you were after Timmy's bar."

"You were dumb lucky that day," muttered Skillman.

I looked at Kerry, whose face was still in her hands.

196

"That's why you called the cops and blew the whistle on Skates," I told her. "You had to have a pigeon."

"Two pigeons," remarked Magen.

"Yeah. You did a good job, Kerry. I thought you were trying to help me."

"I was." A barely audible murmur. She raised up her tearful eyes to look at me. "I was trying to help you stay out of it."

There was something else I didn't understand. How did Magen shoot James with his own gun? James must have known when Magen walked in that it meant trouble.

"How'd you get James's gun?" I asked him.

"I didn't."

"What?"

Kerry began to cry again.

So she *had* been there when James got it.

The scenario played itself out in my mind one last time. Kerry came down to James's apartment after phoning him. James the sappy St. Bernard was so happy to see her that he didn't notice her lift his gun from the desk.

Then Magen came in.

"Why, Kerry?" I asked miserably.

She couldn't speak. Then, "I didn't want it to happen. I didn't think it would. But when it did . . . Eddie, believe me . . . after that, there was nothing I could do. I couldn't get out!"

"From then on you had to do what Magen said."

She nodded soundlessly.

"So it was you who took the gun to Walsh's and planted it in Skates's desk."

Nothing from her.

I looked at Magen. "What now?" I asked rather dopily.

In reply, Magen reached a hand behind him and

opened the door to his office. He backed in, keeping the gun pointed at me.

"Come on," he said.

I was deciding whether to obey him when a rough shove from behind decided it for me. I went sprawling into Magen's carpeted office, with the big, scale-model, chrome-and-glass Magen Building on display in the middle.

Skillman came in behind me and locked the door. I could hear Kerry crying hysterically behind the door to her office.

"Get the crate," Magen shot at Skillman.

I saw it then, in the corner, a wooden crate that looked about the right size to have held the Magen Building model. Magen backed toward a wall and pressed a button. I realized then it was a private elevator. Leading to the basement, no doubt.

I saw the wooden crate, which Skillman was dragging from the corner.

A man my size, doubled over, would fit nicely inside the wooden crate. Then, down the private elevator to the basement, and probably to a landfill somewhere, where I would become a permanent part of the city dump.

I hadn't been properly terrified until then because I couldn't see how they were going to get me out through a busy office in the middle of the day. Now, I saw, and a desperate panic surged through me.

There was no time left to think. Skillman was dragging the case toward me. Magen stood there with an automatic pointed at me. Which one?

I ducked behind the glass-and-chrome Magen Building model and shoved it toward Magen as hard as I could.

Blash! An explosion from the automatic and a splintering of glass as the model shattered and crashed forward.

And then Skillman was on me from behind. I went down on my knees and doubled my head down to the floor, hoping his lunge would carry him over me. He went sprawling over me onto the carpet on his hands and knees in front of me.

I knew I had only one shot, and the target was inviting. Quicker than I can say it, it flashed through my mind that I owed him for that dive under the garage door, and for that swinging iron wrecker's ball that buried my Mustang.

You remember Jim Turner, the old New York Jets placekicker who kicked straight ahead, unlike the soccer-style kickers do now?

I put everything I had into it and kicked a field-goal into Skillman's crotch as he sprawled before me on his hands and knees.

"Ahhhhhhhrrrrrghhhhh!"

And he went flat on his face. And then doubled up in a fetal position holding his groin, something like the way James Kelly had looked after he got it.

Only then did I realize there had been nothing more from Konrad Magen. The Magen Building model, now splattered into broken glass, lay toppled over against the elevator.

Magen was under it, blood pouring from his throat.

32

I REMEMBER A friend once asking me what it was like not to have a job like everyone else. I reminded him that I was a reporter. "Huh," he sneered, "that's not a job."

He was right, in a way. Being a reporter somehow seems like less than a real job, and a lot more. You roll along living other people's lives and forget when Christmas comes, and you even forget to take vacations.

Ironhead sent me on one that September. I didn't ask for one. I even protested that I had that Romance of Buildings series to do, and that I was ready to do it at last.

"Get out of here," he replied.

So, I went. I don't know if I actually planned it, but I ended up on the Cape again, accompanied by the only person I felt I could put up with.

I'm afraid I would have been rotten company for anyone else. I sat in a cottage in a deserted section of beach up near Truro, and did very little. I read Cicero a little, and drank some beer, but neither very well.

"Nothing is more disgraceful than a wolfish friendship," said my companion.

Yes, Marcus.

And I watched the constellations again, wheeling geometrically through the same sky that Marcus once scanned. That's the way it is when life crowds you too much. You watch the stars and read Marcus Aurelius. "There is no veil over a star," commented my ancient mentor. And added unnecessarily, "And on what a small clod of the whole earth you creep."

I was wallowing in it, all right.

I read on, depending upon Marcus, until he explained to me the definition of calamity. "Smoke and ash and a tale and not even a tale."

Kerry had made no attempt to get away that day. In fact, she even called the police. They found us sitting together in her office, smoking silently. She used the time to tell me about it. I don't know if it made me feel better or worse.

Her father had botched a deal at Magen & Burke that almost ruined the firm and nearly put him and Magen in prison. But Magen still took her in later and set her up in an apartment. She was grateful to him until he began visiting the apartment and demanding to stay overnight.

Then James Kelly had shown up, and Kerry discovered his father had a lease on a piece of property Magen desperately wanted. She introduced James to Magen, he was hired, and the scheme to get the New Dublin Inne was hatched.

On the evening of the murder, Magen came to Kerry's apartment and got her to call James to be sure he was in. She heard Skates there. After Skates left, she went to James's apartment. Kerry knew James had bought the gun—to defend himself against Magen. She got the gun from James's desk, and when Magen came in she gave it to him.

"I never thought he would use it," she told me miserably. "Why did I help? To stop Mr. Magen from coming on to me. It worked better than I thought."

James's murder locked them together. Kerry said she had no choice, then, but to plant the gun on Skates and to call the police. And later when I showed up, she told me what Magen wanted me to hear.

"I tried to stop, Fitz, that first day we met at Madame

Charriere's. I went back and told Mr. Magen I was through. But I was in it by then. So . . . "

So, I had enlisted a Trojan horse who was more of a Greek bearing gifts than my St. Bernard eyes could see.

"I didn't know what he was going to do, Eddie. You must believe that. Every time something more happened . . . I . . . "

You can ponder the stars and read even Marcus Aurelius only so long. Then you have to go back. Ironhead had put other reporters on the story of Lenny Skillman, who was charged in the murder of Duffy. Konrad Magen, charged in the others, was beyond the reach of the District Attorney.

Kerry Burke became a prosecution witness, but I didn't cover that story, either. One of the stories that came out was that Magen had botched that deal at Magen & Burke, and that Mr. Burke hadn't killed himself. Magen had done it for him.

In spite of everything, the Magen Building is going up, only it's going to be called Excelsior Towers. Timmy Kelly's new bar is built right into the corner of the building, and he has a longer lease than before.

I drifted back there eventually, like a homing pigeon I guess, and found Timmy on the job as usual with his nephew Stanley Drennen, who was being groomed to take over one day.

"Ah, Fitz," he said to me, "the world does go around."

"It does, at that."

He introduced me to Stan, and told him I could run a tab as long as it didn't get too outrageous.

"He's one of these hotshot, overpaid *noospaper* reporters," Timmy explained, "and he's always broke."

"You're full of canal water, Timmy."

One day a cab pulled up, and who scurried in but that blot on the face of civilized society.

"Jeez, where ya been?" he demanded, his face set in runaway annoyance. "I ask everybody where's Fitz, which nobody knows! Do I try ta find you from Brooklyn ta the Bronx?"

"I don't know, Skates. Do you?"

"But can I find you?"

"Here I am."

"Okay. Does Skates Stern pay off or not?" And he shoved a $100 bill on the bar.

I had to remind Skates that the hundred—the one I gave Jerry Shapiro, the bartender at Walsh's—had come from his own stash.

"Is Skates a liar?" he demanded.

Well, we drank up the hundred bucks that day and on a few other days, and I found out Skates was now driving a cab. "Until the heat's off."

I told him I might need him because my Mustang had disappeared under an avalanche.

So, Skates Stern is shopping the Bronx car auctions for a car for me. And this time I'm getting something nice, depending on what I can afford.

If you have enjoyed this book and would like to receive details of other Walker mystery titles, please write to:

Mystery Editor
Walker and Company
720 Fifth Avenue
New York, NY 10019